I0607718

THE PROPHECY

The Amulet Saga
Volume Four

by

Avily Jerome

THE PROPHECY
Published by Dragontail Press
PO Box 54550
Phoenix, AZ, 85078

ISBN 978-1-7321879-2-4
Copyright © 2019 by Avily Jerome
Cover art concept by Sarah Collotta
Cover design by Kirk DouPonce, Dog Eared Design

Available in print from your local bookstore, online, or from the author at:
www.avilyjerome.com

For more information on this book and the author visit: www.avilyjerome.com

Brought to you by Avily Jerome
And by Dragontail Press, www.avilyjerome.com

Library of Congress Cataloging-in-Publication Data
Jerome, Avily
The Silver Shores/Avily Jerome 1st ed.

Printed in the United States of America.

For my Wonder Women
Lindsay, Sarah, and Catherine
I thank my God upon every remembrance of you

Acknowledgments

Special thanks to my husband, who supports me financially and emotionally, and who allows me to pursue my passion.

Thanks also to my dad, whose continual support for my writing and my books blesses me beyond words.

Thanks to my mom, who taught me to read and instilled in me an endless love of the written word.

And, of course, thank you to my readers, the ones who are still interested in what's going on in Legerdemain

Table of Contents

Souless
Mountains

Legerdemain

Kirland

hordkopf

Zyan

Brachenridge

Rachdale

Winterborne

Malakai's
Ridge
Mountains

Çadalania

Silver
Shores

Ihwen

Cael

Sunnland

Çinverness

Western
Isles

Spalding

Outlaw's Village

Nynthavin

The daughter of the dragon
Who oversees the land
Will live until the day
The dragons come again

Love she'll never know
A child she'll never have
The kings and queens of fate
Her legacy will show

From the path fate strays
The Lover and the Traitor
When the Solstice Moon shines brightly
And at the Dragon, the Dancer waves

Across the ocean wide
The darkness rises swiftly
Untold power unleashed
Building until that day

The reign of power shifts
Fate in the balance
The weight of choices made
Brings life or the end of all

The child lost arises
To take the power back
A child of the enemy
Begotten then to conquer

When the dragons rise again
When the mountains open wide
When the stones of heaven fall
The world is remade.

When the darkness reigns
Then the hate shall bind
The hearts of one and all
Until the light is found

Those who triumph fall
Those who seek shall find
Those who rule shall serve
The servant, ruler of all

The begotten of the dragons
Beloved of the Creator
Who bears the Dragon Stone
The Deliverer of the World

THE PROPHECY

The Amulet Saga
Volume Four

The Prophecy

Ada pored over the manuscripts, checking and cross-referencing things she hadn't read or thought about in more years than she cared to think about.

The signs were aligned. The time was now. The next year would decide the fate of the nation of Legerdemain. The prophecy would be fulfilled one way or another, but how it played out was still to be determined. If Legerdemain fell, then the prophecy would spell ruin for more than those that lived in the tiny valley country. The whole world would be at risk. Domination by those who craved power and would stop at nothing to get it. Slavery. Death. Famine.

The prophecies were clear that a leader would rise up, but whether that leader was there to save or to destroy depended on things that would happen now.

The queen was pivotal.

This queen, specifically. Ada had seen many kings and queens on Legerdemain's throne, but the choices this queen made would have far-reaching consequences.

She sipped at her tea. Something was off about the flavor, but she ignored it. The new servant had told her it was imported from Sunnland, an expensive delicacy. She didn't like it—she'd stick to her old, trusted, local tea from now on.

She scanned the parchment again.

It was always a risk, telling the subject of a prophecy their role, but the queen needed to know at least a little. She needed to understand the weight of her decisions.

She gathered the relevant manuscripts and made her way to the Council room. She couldn't move as quickly as she used to, and that realization was more frustrating than she liked to admit.

She waved to a passing servant. "Please tell the queen I request to meet with her right away. I have important information for her that I must share right away."

The queen arrived just as Ada finished spreading the manuscripts on the table.

"Majesty, there is something you must know. You know what these are, I presume?"

The queen nodded. "The prophecies, spoken by the first king of Legerdemain, telling of the things that will come to pass at the end of this age."

"Yes and no," Ada said. "The prophecies do tell of the end of the age, but there is more to them than that. Prophecies are not always precise, or linear. More often than not, they are fulfilled in waves, or layers, over time."

The queen nodded her understanding.

"I have seen signs in recent days. The stars aligning, omens appearing, confused visions when I am Seeing—all things that lead me to believe this is a pivotal moment in the unfolding of the prophecy. May I see the Amulet?"

The queen removed a large amethyst set in gold from her neck and handed it to Ada.

Ada traced the words etched into the gold. "Look here. This line, 'Deliverer of the world', is the last line of a much longer prophecy."

"I remember studying it as a child, but no one really knows what it means."

"As with most things, prophecies are easier seen from the other side. But we can watch and be ready." Ada pointed to the text of one of the manuscripts. "This stanza talks about the signs of the sky in winter, how

11

the Dancer will wave to the Dragon. The constellations have not been aligned such in hundreds of years, but last night, they began their orbit into one another's space."

The queen bent down to read the text. "It also says a path diverges—a lover and a traitor. What does that mean? Is the lover the traitor? The path diverges when the snow falls under the solstice moon. What does that mean?"

"I wish I knew. But tonight is the solstice moon, though we can't see it because we're expecting snow."

The queen cocked her head at Ada's dry tone.

"You said there were omens?"

Ada nodded. "Birds flying north, to the mountains, instead of south to escape the cold. Herbs growing out of season. Magical energy feeling dampened, then suddenly charged, with no apparent reason for the surge or slump."

"And visions?" the queen asked.

"This is the most troubling. I don't try to See very often. There's too much potential for harm, both from the energy expended and from Seeing too much and misinterpreting what is Seen. But after the omens, I tried. I saw you, but you were obscured. Your face wiped as though you were a painting that had been smeared until it was no longer recognizable. And again, a pair of scales, a decision waiting to be balanced. One choice will lead to dire consequences, while the other opens up the possibility for salvation, but the future is so gray an blurry, I don't know what the decision is."

"So, I must be very careful of any decision I make in the next days?"

"Or weeks. Possibly even months. And it's impossible to decipher how large or small a decision it may be. The simple act of going for a ride to one of the Villages could set in motion events that lead to catastrophe."

The queen smiled, almost indulgently. "If you can't see the decision, or even how monumental of a decision it might be, how can I possibly know which to choose?"

Ada returned the smile, realizing the impossibility of the choice she had set before the queen.

"Every decision I make, I do with thought and care. My father was a good king, and he trained me well. You are a good advisor, and you have given me more wisdom and training than any queen could expect. You must trust that I will never knowingly make a decision that could lead my people or my country to harm."

A knock sounded at the door and the queen's maid poked her head inside.

"Your Majesty, I have just received word that the envoy from Cadalania is approaching. Your betrothed will be at the gates within the hour."

Her betrothed?

Ada raised an eyebrow.

The queen laughed. "There is nothing to fear, Ada. My betrothed is a kind and wise. This is a decision that will benefit Legerdemain. You have to trust me."

The queen hurried from the room, grabbing her maid's hand on her way out. "Come quickly, you must prepare me to meet my guests."

Ada glanced again at the scrolls. Something wasn't right. A feeling like she hadn't had in a very long time warned her against something that was about to happen. She had to follow the queen. But she couldn't risk the manuscripts being lost or destroyed, and she didn't have time to return them to a safe place.

Behind the tapestry hanging on the wall was a vault, built eons before to hide valuables should the castle ever come under attack. Few had known of its existence, even then, and the knowledge was passed down only to a few select people, namely the reigning monarch in every generation.

Ada moved the tapestry to the side and pressed against the stone that triggered the vault to open. She placed the manuscripts inside, then hurried up to the main hall.

The queen was just returning from having her hair hastily brushed and her cosmetics touched up.

13

Ada shuffled toward her just as the front door clanged open and the soldiers standing guard announced that visitors had arrived.

Ada reached out her hand and started to call out a warning.

A spell hit her from behind, something strong and violent. The magic used was twisted, selfish. And so, so powerful. She fell under the weight of it, crushed by a wave of darkness that pushed on her from all sides, draining her of both magical energy and physical awareness.

She still tried to call out to the queen, but words would not come.

A moment later, the darkness overwhelmed her, and she knew no more.

Terea

"She's waking up." The voice sounded hazy, like it was coming through a blanket. It was a woman's voice, older, but not ancient. It seemed familiar, but she couldn't quite remember who it belonged to.

She opened her eyes, then shut them immediately against the glare of a bright light.

"Terea, can you hear me?" the voice asked.

She blinked again, trying to find the source of the voice... but who was Terea?

Slowly, her eyes adjusted to the glare. She was in a spacious room with stone walls lined with elaborate tapestries. Gold sconces held unlit candles, and a fire blazed in a stone fireplace by the wall.

The bright light streamed in from a tall, glass-paned window framed with heavy, red velvet drapes. She was lying in a bed, covered with a soft, thick blanket, propped up with heavy pillows.

Whoever this room belonged to must be someone of some great importance. So how did she get there?

Three people hovered over her, staring at her with anxious faces. Who were they?

"How are you feeling, Sweetheart?" the woman who'd spoken before asked. She wore an elegant purple dress. Silver-streaked brown hair was pulled into an elaborate bun atop her head, and warm brown eyes, filled with concern, bored into her.

"I... I'm not sure. My head hurts."

"You had a nasty fall," the woman said. "The Healer thinks you'll be fully recovered very soon, however."

The second person, another woman, but this one much younger, nodded. "That's right. I am pleased with your progress so far."

The third person, a man, took her hand. "You have no idea how pleased I am to hear it, my love."

She snatched her hand away. Her head felt thick. Mushy. "I... I think you must have me confused with someone else. I... don't know you."

The first woman, the older one, gasped. "Terea, he is your betrothed."

"I am not Terea."

The other three exchanged worried glances.

The Healer stepped closer and put a hand on her forehead, then held up a yellowish gemstone. Something seemed to travel through the stone, some sort of energy, from the Healer into her.

"I can't sense anything physically amiss, but I have heard of such things after a head injury, your Majesty," the Healer said.

Majesty. Did that mean the older woman was a queen? Or perhaps the Healer was addressing the man. He looked regal enough to be a king, with gold-trimmed cuffs on his deep blue coat and his pointed, oiled beard.

"What can be done?" the older woman asked.

"I will keep trying, but the only thing we can do for now is help her to heal physically and trust that her mind will return in time." The Healer turned and left the room.

She smiled weakly at the older woman. "Thank you for your help... Majesty?"

The woman's eyes clouded. "Terea, do you not know me, either?"

She bit her lip and shook her head. "I'm very sorry. I do not."

"I am your mother."

Her mother?

No, that could not be possible. How the woman could be so confused was a mystery, but she would know her own mother. Wouldn't she?

Then again, her own mother would know her, too. And they all seemed to think she was Terea. Could they be right? Could she be Terea?

The woman claiming to be her mother looked at the man. "Jagur, what shall we do?"

"We will do as the Healer instructed." The man, Jagur, clasped her hand again. "I have no doubt that our love will see her through."

"If only Ada were here," the woman—her mother—sighed.

"Ada is gone." Jagur's voice sounded harsh, angry even. "She abandoned us when we needed her the most, and she stole the kingdom's most valuable treasure when she left. She is a traitor."

Her mother sighed again. "It's still so hard to believe Ada would do such a thing. She had always been such a faithful servant to the crown. To Terea's father."

"The king is gone. Ada took advantage of that and used her position to try to destroy the kingdom."

"It's all so unreal," her mother sighed.

"Do you have another explanation?" Jagur asked.

"No, I don't. I suppose you must be right. It's just so strange. But I know if she were here—and if she weren't a traitor—she would know how to help."

"Well, she isn't, and we must trust the Healer we do have."

Terea looked from one to the other, her mother and Jagur. Who were these people, and if she really was Terea, why could she not remember anything? Anything about herself, about her mother or her betrothed, about her kingdom, about Ada?

Her stomach churned and her vision spotted. She couldn't think. Couldn't feel anything but terror clawing its way through her.

The Healer returned with a cup of some sort of steaming liquid and handed it to Terea. "Drink up," she said. She turned to the others. "We should let her rest for a bit."

Jagur leaned in and kissed her forehead. "Rest well, my love."

His words and the tea soothed her. She could trust him. Somehow she knew that.

18

The older woman squeezed Terea's hand. "I'll be close by if you need me."

"Thank you..." She still couldn't bring herself to call the stranger *mother*. "Thank you, your Majesty."

The woman paused, her head tilted slightly to the side as she studied Terea. "Terea, I'm not the queen. You are."

Betrothed

The hallways and rooms seemed unfamiliar, and yet Terea knew them well. She didn't recognize the tapestries or the turns, but she found her feet following the route from her bed chamber to the dining hall and the throne room almost without thought.

Her betrothed was at her side almost constantly, leaving her only to sleep. He gazed at her with such soulful eyes, she felt as though she should recognize the emotion written there, but she had no memory of him prior to waking up the previous morning.

She must have loved him, or she wouldn't have agreed to marry him, would she?

And yet she could not sense any familiarity, any of the tenderness she would've expected to feel for someone she loved.

Even her mother had begun to feel familiar, like a long lost friend she hadn't seen in years, but with whom she'd always have a connection. But Jagur? There was nothing.

He held her arm and guided her to the Council room, where a group of people who also seemed vaguely familiar but who she couldn't place, sat around a large table. Her mother sat there as well, next to the empty seat at the head of the table. Her mother nodded toward the empty seat.

Terea sat, and Jagur sat on her other side. A man with a dark, gray-streaked beard, seated on the other side of Terea's mother, spoke. "We must discuss what we're going to tell the people," he said.

"What have we already told them?" Terea's mother asked.

Terea smiled. Her mother knew she wouldn't remember anything that had been discussed, and was helping to save her from embarrassment.

"They know she was injured during the attack on the castle, and that she will need some time in seclusion, but they do not know the nature or extent of her injuries."

"And what are the nature of her injuries?" a woman at the far end of the table asked. She looked at Terea, not any of the others.

Terea opened her mouth, but found no words sufficient to express her situation. She didn't even recognize the woman, so how could she begin to know what the woman was looking for?

Jagur took her hand. "May I?"

She nodded.

"The queen is physically in good health. The Healer expects her to make a full recovery. However," he paused and squeezed her hand. "One of her injuries was a blow to the head, and while the Healer believes there is no lasting damage, it seems to have affected her memory."

"Affected her memory how?" the woman asked.

Jagur paused, as though not sure how to much to reveal.

Terea squeezed his hand. These were her advisors, the people she trusted, or so she was told. They'd agreed to be completely honest. "I can't remember anything," she said.

The woman looked at Terea. "Nothing?"

Terea nodded. "I'm afraid not. I don't remember anything before yesterday morning. I didn't even know my name until they told me. I feel as though I should know you all, but I can't quite reach the place in my mind where those memories should be. I don't even remember my mother or my betrothed."

The woman raised an eyebrow. "Your betrothed."

Jagur stood. "My apologies. I am Lord Jagur of Cadalania. I have only just arrived. Her Majesty and I met on her travels last year. We have been corresponding ever since. We made our engagement official when I arrived a week ago."

21

Terea gulped. Was this shy she had no memories of him? Because they'd been apart so long?

The woman at the other end voiced Terea's thoughts. "Convenient, that your arrival coincides with a head injury which caused her Majesty to forget everything and thus render her unable to vouch for you."

"Don't be absurd," Terea's mother said. "I saw them together when he arrived, and that evening Terea told me she had an important announcement to make at the next Council meeting."

"I don't like it," the woman said.

Terea's mother raised a hand. "I understand your concern. I had the same questions. But Jagur has produced correspondence between himself and Terea, written in her hand, and sealed with her seal, and her maid showed me the letters she received from him, as well. I am convinced he is who he says he is and that my daughter's love for him, as well as her engagement, is legitimate."

"I would like to see those documents myself," the woman said.

"Certainly," Jagur said, then quickly turned to Terea. "That is, if you have no objection?"

Terea nodded slowly. She'd like to see them for herself, first. But she saw no reason to keep the truth from them. And she had no reason to believe Jagur was anything other than straightforward. He had been nothing but kind and devoted to her.

And yet… how could she even trust her own emotions, when they were based on only one day of experience?

"What does Ada have to say?" the man to her mother's left asked.

"I'm afraid…" Terea's mother took a deep breath. "I'm afraid Ada is missing. We don't know yet if she was harmed or killed in the attack or whether…"

"Or whether she was responsible for them," Jagur finished for her.

Prisoner

Ada traced the walls with her fingertips for at least the thousandth time, but of course, nothing had changed. It was impenetrable, even for her. That was the point. Built beneath the castle at the founding of Legerdemain to house prisoners like herself, to keep them from being able to access or wield magic.

Stone walls, magically sealed together so no root could edge its way inside. Completely dry, no drips of water trickling in from anywhere, so nothing, not even moss or fungus, could grow.

How had they even known about it? It hadn't been used in hundreds of years.

But the how was irrelevant. They'd caught her unaware. Hit her from behind using a powerful spell. Drugged her, using an unfamiliar herb. It was nothing she'd encountered before—she would've recognized it if it had been. They'd put it in her tea. Even then, she'd felt something was off about the flavor, but she hadn't realized. She'd been too trusting. Hadn't thought there was anything to fear.

By the time she felt the effects of the drug, it was too late. No time to find an antidote, even if she'd known what she was dealing with.

She felt the magic going first. Her ability to sense it, to draw on it, muted, then fading completely. Her head grew heavy and she couldn't think clearly. She'd stumbled toward the queen, trying to warn her, but soon her limbs stopped responding, as well, and she'd been powerless to even sense, let alone combat, the spell that made her collapse in the hallway.

She'd heard footsteps coming toward her and tried to moan for help, but even her voice refused to obey.

When she'd awoken, she'd found herself trapped here in this forgotten cell, that no one except for herself and apparently her captors knew existed, and from which there was no escape.

Who were they? The mysterious attackers who knew enough to incapacitate her before ever attempting to attack the kingdom? Terea was expecting her betrothed to arrive. He'd sent word that he would be arriving before the autumn festival. Ada had been wary, always suspicious. She'd had her spies and the castle guards on high alert for any sign of betrayal. She didn't really expect it—Terea had good sense—but she would not let a troop of soldiers from another land enter without doing her due diligence to keep the kingdom safe.

But she'd been attacked before the Cadalanin and his retinue had ever arrived.

There must be a spy in the palace. But who? Who knew enough about the workings of the castle, about their security, and most importantly, about Ada herself to be able to attack her without anyone being the wiser?

And the worst part was, Ada had no way of knowing what happened next. No way to know if the queen was dead, if the country had been overrun, if…

No, she could not indulge in ifs. She had to find a way out.

A guard came once a day to empty her chamber pot, replacing it with a new one so he wouldn't have to return until the following day, and delivering her meal. Dried meat and vegetables cooked so thoroughly, not a trace of magical energy remained in them. Enough to keep her alive, but sap her of all strength.

The guard thumped down the passageway toward her cell. He opened the window panel to deliver her daily meal.

"Please," she rasped, handing him her pot and the previous day's plate. "I am so ill. Couldn't I have just a little tea?"

"I'm not authorized to deliver anything but what is ordered."

"Surely a little tea for a sickly old woman is not too great a request. Please. Ask the queen. I'm certain she would not be so cruel."

The guard shoved her plate inside and handed her the fresh pot. "I'll see," he grunted.

He slammed the panel shut and thumped back down the passageway.

He didn't react to her mention of the queen. What did that mean? Was the queen still alive? Was she in danger? Or did someone else sit upon the throne?

An hour later, the guard returned with a cup of very weak tea.

"Thank you," Ada said, but her voice was lost in the clanging echo of the door that kept her sealed off from him.

She inhaled the aroma. Valerian root and poppy. Clever. Both herbs would suppress her ability to sense magic. Good thing she had no intention of consuming it.

She tore a small strip of cloth from her worn, dirty sheet, then poked a hole in the straw mat she slept on. The straw was long-since dead and drained of magical strength, but it would rot and provide a fertile base for other things.

Using the cloth on the outside and the straw on the inside, she built a nest of sorts and very carefully poured the tea over it, breaking up the straw and adding a little more at a time until all the tea was absorbed and none of the liquid wasted.

She set the nest in a corner of the room, behind her straw mat, and set the cup with her dinner plate on her lap to eat.

She let her voice come through just a little stronger when the guard came back the next day. "Thank you. Do you think perhaps I might have more tea?"

The guard made no promises, but the next day he returned with more tea when he brought her dinner.

She carefully poured it into her nest. Already she could sense a colony of mold beginning to grow. In another week, she would have enough growth to start drawing on the magic, channeling energy back and forth to strengthen both herself and her little garden.

But so much could happen in a week.

26

What was going on in the palace? What had happened to Terea? And would it be too late to put things right when she finally escaped this dungeon?

Memory

Terea sat at the table in her sitting room and pored over the letters to and from Jagur, trying to grasp any connection to them, to him—to herself.

Her maid, a woman named Arna—yet another woman Terea felt no familiarity for nor connection to—sat beside her.

"I remember when you wrote this one," Arna said. "You had just learned that your friend, Whytni, had passed away."

"Who was Whytni?"

"Whytni was a member of Parlaiment, and a very wise woman. She was the one who helped you most in your transition to queen, even more than Ada. You cried. See, this is where you blotted your tears, but decided to send the letter anyway, so as not to waste parchment."

Terea studied the page. The way the smeared ink resembled a flower—a lilac, her favorite…

She gasped and looked up at Arna. "I remembered something. Lilacs are my favorite flower."

Arna smiled. "That's wonderful news, Majesty. I'll tell the Healer at once." She stood and hurried away.

Terea stared at the page again. Now that she'd connected a memory to it, the whole page felt familiar. She didn't remember Whytni, but she remembered the sense of loss she'd experienced when writing the letter, the gaping emptiness burrowing deep into her soul.

Arna and the Healer returned a few minutes later.

"Good morning, Majesty," the Healer said. "I understand you've remembered something."

"Terea nodded. "Lilacs. They're my favorite flower."

"That's very good. It means our treatments are working. Have some tea."

Terea took the cup and sipped the steaming tea. "How did Whytni die?" she asked.

"She was ill," Arna said. "A disease no one recognized. Not a plague, for no one else contracted it."

Arna's eyes darted around the room and her voice dropped. "Some said her ailment was... magical."

Terea coughed, nearly spitting out her tea. "Who would do that to her? And why? Did she have enemies?"

"I do not know, your Majesty. She was your closest friend and most trusted confidant. If she had an enemy, you are the one who would've known."

Terea clenched her eyes shut. Why couldn't she remember?

Everything, even the lilac, just felt so... fuzzy. Ever since she'd been awake, she felt like she'd been walking around with a towel over her head. Sometimes something would spark a memory, like the lilac-shaped water spot had, but it always felt so muted, like trying to listen to someone talking underwater.

She reached for the feeling the letter had evoked, grasping to hold onto it, but it was already fading.

She remembered seeing the ink blot, and she knew it meant something, but she could no longer feel it.

She knew lilacs were her favorite flower, but she knew it in the way that she knew the sky was blue or cats were soft. The knowledge didn't impact her personally—she just didn't care.

The information was meaningless.

She pulled her mind back to focus. What had they been talking about? Oh, yes. Her friend.

Was Whytni even real? Did their friendship matter? How could it, when Terea had no memory of her at all?

But there was something important, something she needed to know. The knowledge tickled the back of her mind. What was it?

She looked at the Healer. "If Whytni's illness was magical, why couldn't you help her?"

"I would have, if I had been here. That was before I came. But I will say one thing—creating a disease that only affects the intended victim requires a level of magical skill that few can boast. And curing it would take an equal amount of skill. If you asked me, I would say the one most likely to have performed such a spell would be the one who would naturally be called in to cure it. It would've been a perfect ruse—pretend to cure, while all the while making it worse, ensuring the spell did what it was intended to."

The Healer refilled Terea's tea, then swept from the room.

Terea stared after her. It made sense that a Healer would have the skills to counteract her own arts. Who was the Healer before this one came?

She knew it—the name was just out of reach, hidden in a murky corner of Terea's mind.

The other Healer must have had a reason if she'd been the one to kill Whytni. What reason? Whytni had been Terea's friend and confidant—perhaps she had figured out something the previous Healer wanted to keep silent. But what? And how could she find out, when, of the two people who knew, one was dead and the other missing?

She had to find the previous Healer.

She had to find Ada.

Yes, that was her name. Ada had the answers.

But how could she find someone she didn't even remember? Especially when she was having trouble recalling why it was even important?

Her eyes drooped. She was tired. So, so tired. All she wanted was to sleep.

The door opened and Jagur came in. "Hello, my love. Would you care to take a walk around the garden before lunch?"

Terea smiled at him. He was so handsome. And kind.

30

She knew why she had loved him, even if she didn't remember feeling that way.

She wasn't sure she loved him now, but she would. If she didn't remember, then she would fall in love with him again.

She held out her hand and let him help her up. "I would love to."

Parliament

The Council room echoed with Terea's footsteps. She'd been too nervous when she was here before to pay much attention to the room itself. Vaulted ceilings disappeared into shadows high above. Lamps flickered from gilded sconces on the walls, making the figures on the tapestries seem to move.

"Here, Majesty," Arna said, directing her to the high-backed wooden chair at the head of the table.

"Why here?" Terea asked.

Arna gave her a concerned look. "Because you're the queen. You have a meeting with Parliament today, to decide the best course for making decisions until you're well." She indicated the chair. "But this is still your rightful place."

"No, I mean why this room? There are no windows, and it was like a maze to get in here."

"Security, Majesty," Arna said. "In times of war, it was important to ensure no one could eavesdrop or gain access to the monarch. No windows prevents anyone from using magic to listen in, and the winding hallways make it an easy room to protect."

Terea nodded, but the uneasiness didn't leave the pit of her stomach. It might make it easy to protect, but it also made it easy to trap someone.

A room with no escape.

She walked slowly toward the wall, where a series of tapestries seemed to tell a story.

The first showed a battle scene. At least five armies were represented in the fighting warriors and bodies strewn across the plain, differentiated by their physical features as well as their armor and banners.

The next tapestry showed a handful of people, warriors and civilians together, from all the different peoples on the war tapestry, walking a long path, as though embarking on a great journey.

After that, a tapestry showing a wide field populated by strange beasts with leathery skin like a lizard's, but wings like a bat.

The fourth tapestry showed a man kneeling before the beasts, while a beautiful woman with flowing golden hair and piercing blue eyes placed a purple gem on a gold chain around his neck. The gem—that was familiar. And important. She knew it, deep inside her, but she couldn't remember why.

Terea turned to Arna. "What do these mean?"

"They are said to tell of the founding of our nation, but I don't know the story well."

Terea turned her gaze back to the fourth tapestry.

Something about the gold-haired woman intrigued her. Who was she?

The lamp flickered, changing the shadows for a moment. The purple gemstone seemed to glow, and the gold-haired woman's eyes changed.

For an instant, it felt as though the woman on the tapestry looked straight at Terea.

Find me.

Terea gasped and stepped back, blinking.

"What is it, Majesty? Are you feeling ill?" Arna asked.

Terea stared at the tapestry, a perfectly ordinary piece of woven cloth, and at the woman whose gold hair and blue eyes had been muted by years and dust.

"I... I'm fine. I just felt a little woozy for a moment."

Anna handed her the flask of medicinal tea that the Healer insisted she have on hand at all times. "You'll want to make sure you are at your best. Parliament will be here soon."

Terea took a swig of the tea and almost instantly felt her nerves begin to calm.

She took her sat at the head of the table and adjusted the diadem on her head.

A few moments later, the first of the members of Parliament arrived.

A grizzled man with warm brown eyes and a kind smile entered first. She recognized him from the Council meeting. Parliament consisted of some of the Council members and some nobles who were not on the Council. Her mother had explained that while the Council existed to give advice to the throne, they still answered to it, while Parliament existed to keep the monarchy in balance, and could overrule the king or queen if they deemed it necessary.

The man took her hand. "It's good to see you feeling like yourself again, Majesty."

"Thank you," she smiled. She searched her memory for the instructions Arna had given her, the list of names and descriptions, and what Arna could remember of personal details.

This had to be Lord Cristofer. He had been her father's best friend. He was fiercely loyal, but not afraid to make his opinion known.

The others filed in, each expressing their pleasure at her recovery.

Lady Merithine, Lady Linzy, Sir Ian, Sir Lein, and Lady Genevieve. Lady Linzy was on the Council as well as Parliament—she'd been the one to raise suspicions about Terea's engagement to Jagur.

When they were all seated, Sir Cristofer addressed Terea. Your Majesty, during your illness, we have not been idle. We have uncovered a network of spies within our borders, all with ties back to Cadalania."

Terea's throat tightened. Cadalania. Where Jagur was from.

"We believe the King of Cadalania to be unaware of any plots against our sovereignty, but the information we've been able to glean suggests that someone from within their borders is manipulating events in order to undermine our rule."

Sir Cristofer placed a gnarled hand over hers. "This may be difficult to accept, Majesty, but it's possible someone within your fiancé's circle of advisors is using his connection to you to further their own agenda."

Terea nodded, suppressing a sigh of relief that Jagur himself was not implicated in the plot.

"What do you know of Lord Jagur's retinue?" Sir Cristofer asked.

"I'm afraid not much," Terea said. "With my... illness, I have not been able to do the due diligence I should."

"It's quite all right, Majesty. We will continue to search. In the meantime, I must advise that you keep all matters of state private, even from him. We don't know who might try to manipulate his relationship with you, or what information they might use against you."

Terea nodded. She supposed she must trust Jagur, else she would not have agreed to marry him. But right now she didn't trust herself. She didn't even know enough to know what kinds of information might be of interest to foreign powers.

One thing still weighed on her, however. "What of the search for Ada?" she asked.

"Still no leads, Majesty."

Terea clenched her lips. They needed to find Ada. It was important. She didn't know why, but she could feel the pull every time Ada's name was mentioned. "One more thing... Are we certain she was the power behind the invasion?"

Sir Cristofer eyed her. There was wisdom behind his gaze, and a hint of something she couldn't quite place when he said, "All evidence suggests that it is so."

Embroidery

Terea paced her bedchamber. She wanted to be alone, but someone was always with her. Either Arna, or Jagur, or the Healer. Sometimes her mother.

She wanted to think, to search her mind for her memories. They had to be somewhere, didn't they? Buried, not erased. Or so the tiny impressions that forced their way through the fog of her mind seemed to indicate.

Or so she hoped. If she could just concentrate long enough, she thought she could get to them. Every now and then, a flash of something would come to her, but it was gone before she had a chance to grasp it. Even at night, Arna slept in the room with her. And the tea the Healer gave her to help her rest worked beautifully. Her mind grew foggy almost as soon as she lay her head on her pillow, and her thoughts turned to porridge.

"Majesty, can I help you with something?" Arna asked.

Terea shook her head. "I'm just thinking."

"You know the Healer said not to overextend yourself," Arna said.

"I'm not. I'm just trying to remember."

"The Healer said your memories would come back on their own. Trying too hard could injure your mind more."

"I know. I'm trying to be careful. Perhaps there is something else I could do. Did I enjoy anything mundane before? Embroidery or art? What did I do with my time?"

Arna seemed to be at a loss. "You were the queen. You didn't do much frivolous activity. But I know how to embroider. I could teach you."

Terea nodded. "Yes, thank you."

Arna showed her the stitches. The work seemed to come naturally. Perhaps she had learned to do it sometime before, and her fingers remembered the motions. The best part, however, was that while she was focused on a cloth and thread, no one asked her to stop thinking. They all—her mother, the Healer, Arna, Jagur—told her not to over-exert her mind or try too hard to think. They all agreed that would only delay her healing.

But she couldn't stop searching for the answers. They didn't know how it felt to be a stranger in their own home. To have people looking to them for answers they couldn't give. To not recognize the person staring at them from the mirror.

They didn't understand.

She couldn't just lie back and let her mind remain a swampland. She only felt useful, productive, when she was making connections, dredging up bits and pieces of the things she knew and connecting them, trying to figure out how they fit into the life they told her she had. People she should know, or remember, and how they impacted her life.

Whytni, her friend and confidant. She'd died from a mysterious illness. The Healer had suggested that Ada, the former palace Healer, was to blame. A murder designed to look like a natural death.

Something about that pulled on her. After Whytni died, other things had happened. A memory tickled the back of Terea's mind. Something about Whytni's death had triggered other things—spells, enchantments—that broke open at her death. Like magical protections against murder.

What were they?

Terea wanted to ask, but she couldn't bring herself to ask her mother or Arna. Jagur wouldn't know—he wasn't here at the time. He'd only just arrived. But every time she tried to bring up something that her mind tried to grasp on to, her mother and Arna scolded her for taxing herself. She needed to rest to heal. She needed to relax and give her body and mind time to rejuvenate.

They were right, of course. Every time she spent too much time thinking, the memories seemed to fade even more, drifting away from her until they were threads she couldn't grasp. Every time she tried to cling to a flash of something, it disappeared, seeming even more distant than it had been when she tried to listen to it.

So she sat and focused on her embroidery, but her mind wandered back to Whytni. She'd trusted Whytni. Whytni tried to help her. She'd been killed.

What was she trying to help Terea do? How had she threatened Ada with her knowledge or help? She must have done something to make Ada kill her.

A half-formed image stole its way into Terea's mind. Whytni, a middle-aged woman, said she'd found something out. A plot, to undermine Terea's rule.

Who was behind it? Ada?

No, that wasn't right. Ada wasn't the enemy. Terea didn't know how she knew, couldn't place any reason why Ada was trustworthy, but she knew, deep inside, that Ada was not the one undermining the kingdom.

It was someone else. And Whytni knew. Whytni had found evidence. What evidence? Had she shown it to Terea? Or had she died first?

How had Whytni known?

What had she found out?

And why couldn't Terea think? Tears formed in her eyes, and she blinked them back. The fog that clouded her mind made her feel so… useless. She couldn't be a queen when she couldn't put two thoughts together. She couldn't rule a nation when she had no idea who she was.

Kirland.

The country that bordered Legerdemain to the west.

Whytni had said something about Kirland. But that couldn't be— Terea's mother was from Kirland. They were at peace. She must be misremembering. Again.

Terea stabbed the cloth with her needle, her stitches uneven and as violent as her broken mind.

"My love, what is going on?"

Terea jumped and glanced up to see Jagur hovering over her. "Nothing, I—I just am realizing that I can't even remember how to do simple tasks like embroidering, and it is frustrating."

"Of course it is. That is why you should not try too hard to do these things. I'm here. I'll take care of you. You don't need to do anything. I will take care of you, my love."

He handed her a cup of tea and she took a sip.

Thank goodness he was here. What would she do without him? Already she felt calmer. He took such good care of her. She could hardly remember now why she'd been so upset a moment before.

Spies

"How is the investigation coming along?" Lord Jagur asked.

Terea deferred to him. Though technically she should be running the meeting, Jagur always seemed to know just what to say.

They sat in the Council room, along with just a couple of members of the Council, but not all of them.

Captain Tyear, the captain of Terea's personal guard, gave his report. "Two new spies were uncovered, my Lord," he said. "These were men from the North Village, one a miner and one the owner of a tavern. They were contacted by a man they cannot identify, told that the queen is not competent to reign. The story seems to be consistent—a descendant of the royal line has been found, a man who was raised in the East Village and knows the needs of the people, but a merchant who is also educated and understands the law and government. With the help of Cadalanian allies, he would take the throne. Given the queen's poor health, they were told it was in the country's best interest to depose the queen."

Terea gulped. She couldn't be sure that wasn't true. She didn't remember what kind of queen she was. Maybe the people had good reason to object to her reign. Perhaps they would be better off with her relative the merchant.

"What were they told to do?" Jagur asked.

"More of the same," Tyear said. "Keep a record of everything they heard, both in support of the queen and in support of the idea of deposing her. They were to keep a record and inform their recruiter of who was on their side and who still supported the queen."

"But they had no way to contact this person? They can give no indication of who he was or where to find him?"

"No, sir."

Jagur sighed deeply, his annoyance clearly evident on his face.

Terea squeezed his hand to soothe him and turned to Captain Tyear. "What of this merchant, the one who is supposed to be my successor?"

Captain Tyear shook his head. "I do not know, Majesty. We have interviewed all the merchants in the East Village, and we have begun interviewing those in the other villages. No one admits to being the supposed heir. Moreover, we cannot find anyone with a valid claim to the throne. Either he doesn't know his true heritage and he is being set up by someone else, or he is an illegitimate heir, and so we have no way of proving his true identity."

Terea sighed. She would have loved to meet this elusive relative.

"Very well," Jagur said. "Continue your search. Keep us informed if you uncover any evidence that points to this usurper."

"With all due respect," Sir Cristofer said, "I'm not certain there is a usurper."

Jagur raised a disdainful brow.

"Oh, I'm not saying there isn't a descendant of the throne somewhere," Sir Cristofer said, waving his hand absently. "There very well might be. But I don't think he is trying to set himself up as king. Until a month ago, our own network had heard no rumblings of unrest, nor any indication of anyone else making a claim to the throne."

"With all due respect," Jagur said, his lip curling in a sneer, "your *network* allowed spies to infiltrate the castle and attack the queen. The queen's trusted advisor is believed to be at the heart of this."

"That is precisely my point," Sir Cristofer said, seemingly unfazed by Jagur's disdain. "Any citizen is free to enter the castle grounds. They are free to bring concerns or complaints or claims of any sort. Anyone in our kingdom could have come in without challenge. They didn't need to use your retinue as a diversion. Ada would have known this—she would not have needed your visit as an excuse. I believe Ada was set up. Her position of influence makes her a perfect target—anyone might assume she wanted more power for herself, and a monarch under her complete control."

"Exactly!" Jagur smacked the table with his hand. "Isn't that where all the evidence points?" He directed that toward Captain Tyear.

"We still have not been able to find Ada," Tyear said. "She seems to have disappeared completely. If she were behind this plot, we should have found her hiding somewhere, or found someone who had seen her, at least. I have found no evidence to suggest that she is even in the country."

"Ada has been a loyal servant of the throne for longer than even I know. She has more power than any of you realize. If she disappeared, she is either dead or otherwise incapacitated. She would not leave the throne unprotected, and she would have no need of a puppet-king. That is why I believe there is more here than an insurrection. I believe foreign powers are at play."

"To what end?" Jagur asked. "Legerdemain cannot be ruled by a foreign power. Who other than a relative would have the means to usurp the throne? And who other than a trusted advisor to manipulate events? Yes, I've heard the rumors that Cadalania is at fault, but I assure you, it isn't true. Cadalania wishes to be allied with Legerdemain. We want peace. It must be someone who is Legerdemainian."

"If there is a potential successor out there, I believe he is being set up as a puppet by someone else," Sir Cristofer insisted. "Many of the spies have connections to Cadalania, some are even fully Cadalanian. We need to find the one behind this whole plot. Finding the claimant to the throne may or may not even matter if we don't find the person responsible for setting him up."

"I have seen no evidence that this is the case," Jagur said.

"And you are not the king," Sir Cristofer returned. "Our country's defense is not your main priority."

Jagur bolted to his feet. "How dare you. Her Majesty's wellbeing is my only concern."

Sir Cristofer remained as impassive as ever. "Be that as it may, the country's leadership and politics are not. Any claimant to the throne would still need the approval of Parliament, so any attempt to usurp would be difficult by force. However, if the claimant made a reasonable defense, Parliament might actually agree. A foreign power would not necessarily know this, however, and thus he might feel that force and subterfuge are the most effective means to securing the throne. So again I say, we need to find the power behind the insurrection, not just the supposed successor to the throne."

Jagur still bristled, but he sat down.

Terea laid a hand on his arm. Her head swam with all the arguing, the plots and counter-plots, but she needed to assure her people she was still fit to be queen, at least until a better ruler was found. She addressed the Council. "I agree with your assessment. Let us keep looking before we condemn a relative, especially if his claim is valid."

Rat

Felyp spent the first week after the arrest hiding in the cellars beneath the castle's large kitchen. He nibbled bits of leftovers from the trays after everyone else had gone to bed and only the hounds lounged in front of the fireplace.

He watched the servants, learned their routines and the shortcuts they used to serve the queen and other nobility without being visible or getting in the way.

He overheard gossip, but it was hard to put much together.

The queen and her consort were searching out spies, people they believed were behind the invasion.

Fools.

The General would know what to do.

But where was the General?

Felyp hadn't heard him named among those known to have been arrested, not that those arrests meant anything. Fools making assumptions. Using any excuse, from country of origin to the slightest hearsay of disloyalty, to make accusations. Confirming a plot by Sunnland and Cadalania against the throne, and no objective source to tell them they were wrong.

But if they had arrested the General, wouldn't it have been publicly proclaimed?

He would be known to be a Cadalanian official. He would be a perfect scapegoat for whatever plots they wished to pin upon him.

So why hadn't Felyp heard anything?

When the General didn't surface after a few more days, Felyp knew he'd have to do some searching. He stole a servant's uniform so he could walk unnoticed through the passageways. He carried trays or bags of laundry most of the time, and walked quickly, with determined steps, so others would assume he was hard at work.

The queen met almost daily with the Council, and though Felyp had brought food once or twice, he could not get in to hear.

The same thing with the throne room and the queen's hearings with her subjects. He could never quite get close enough to overhear anything useful.

Perhaps, if he could just get close to the queen…

But she was always flanked by her maid and her consort.

Her consort.

Who was he?

Felyp knew the man's name—Lord Jagur—but who *was* he? And how had he risen to such a position of power?

The General had never mentioned Lord Jagur when they'd made their plans.

A foreign man, guiding the queen's actions, and she following him almost blindly.

Why? And how did the General not know of him?

How did the General not see it coming? And what was the General planning to do now? Did he have a plan?

Of course. He always had a plan. But where was he? Was he hiding in hallways and cellars, like Felyp? Or was he gone from this place? How would Felyp know what the next step was? What if he never found the General?

No. Thoughts like that did no good. The General had a plan. He must. And if he had a plan, he would need Felyp and the others to carry it out.

He had to find a way to listen in on the queen's hearings. Even better, her Council meetings. Or perhaps he should start with Lord Jagur. There was more to that man than he let on.

If Felyp could ingratiate himself with Lord Jagur, then he might get something useful.

He went back to the kitchen and prepared a tray of exotic foods to tempt Lord Jagur, then made his way toward Lord Jagur's private chambers.

He stopped in the hall just outside Lord Jagur's rooms. Lord Jagur shouted something, but his voice was muffled, coming from inside his suite.

Felyp glanced around to ensure no one was coming, then pressed his ear to the keyhole.

Somehow, that made it harder to hear, like Lord Jagur was in another room. His bed chamber, rather than the front sitting room of his suite, perhaps? But if that was so, how had Felyp heard him through the stone walls?

Was there perhaps a chink somewhere that allowed sound to travel? He set the tray of food on the floor by the door, then padded softly down the hallway.

The voice grew louder again. "You said you had it under control," Lord Jagur growled.

"It *is* under control." A woman's voice. "But you can't have it both ways. Either total submission, or a reasonable amount of thought to convince the others she's coherent."

Felyp strained his ears. The sound was coming from… the rafters? He looked up, trying to see anything in the shadowed heights, but only dust and shadows looked down on him.

The voices were muffled again, incoherent. But the sound was definitely coming from above.

He glanced down the hallway again. No one was near. There were no tapestries here, but the stones jutted out in places, making sufficient hand- and footholds.

Taking a deep breath, he gripped a small pock in the wall with one hand and stuck his toes in another. Bit by bit, he scaled the wall until he could reach the rafter overhead and pull himself up. Dust clouded around him, undisturbed for untold years until he'd climbed up. He fought not to cough or sneeze and betray his presence.

In the future, he'd remember to tie a scarf around his nose and mouth to keep from breathing the dust.

The voices were much clearer now, and Felyp moved carefully along the rafters in that direction.

There, a few feet down, was a crack of light coming through from the other side of the wall.

As he got closer, Felyp realized it wasn't just a crack, it was a small trapdoor, wedged open just a bit.

"Consider it done, my lord," the woman snapped.

A moment later, a door slammed, then the door to the hallway opened. Felyp couldn't turn from his precarious position on the rafters to see who she was, so he held very still until her footsteps faded. Shen she was gone, he crept the last little bit to the trapdoor and nudged it open.

As he suspected, it opened onto the rafters in Lord Jagur's room.

This was good. He could now see everything that went on in here.

Did all the rooms have these doorways? He hoped so. That would give him a tremendous advantage.

Now, he would be able to find the General, if he was anywhere to be found.

Treaty

"We must discuss the treaty," Lady Linzy said. "That is why he came, isn't it? Or was it just to seduce our queen?"

Terea squeezed Jagur's hand. She was sure Lady Linzy didn't mean to be rude.

"I have it here," Lord Jagur said, handing over a scroll of parchment. He didn't seem the least put out by Lady Linzy's accusation. "Already signed by his Majesty, King Vacen of Cadalania. It increases the importation of wine and crops, and adds a program of mutual learning. Every year, one Cadalanian noble will come to Legerdemain for instruction in mining, magic, and art, while one Legerdemainian noble will come to Cadalania for instruction in wine making, politics, and culture."

Terea smiled at him. He was so handsome, with his oiled beard and calm, confident demeanor.

Lady Linzy scrutinized the scroll. Sir Cristofer leaned over so he could see it, as well.

Terea looked up. The shadows shifted on the tapestries again. The golden-haired woman stared at her, seeming almost to shake her head.

Terea shuddered. The tapestry was a priceless piece of her nation's history, but she might have to have it taken down.

"The part I'm concerned about is this," Lady Linzy pointed to a section about two thirds of the way through the scroll, "where it locks Legerdemain into being allies even in times of war."

Lord Jagur waved a hand in the air. "It's standard wording for all peace treaties. Friends in peace, allies in war."

"Legerdemain has always been politically neutral," Sir Cristofer said. "In all our history, we have never sided with any other nation against another in any conflict."

"We are not at war," Lord Jagur insisted. "We have similar treaties with our other neighbors. The treaty will expire long before there is any hint of ill will between our nations."

Terea reached for the scroll. "May I?"

Lady Linzy passed it to her.

She read through it, slowly. The weight of her missing memories seemed to press in all around her. She had to think. Why couldn't she think?

She swallowed and forced her eyes to move along the page, her mind to comprehend what it absorbed. "It's not just standard wording," she said. "It specifically conscripts magic users to come to Cadalania's aid in times of war. I don't know that I feel comfortable signing this. Making hasty decisions in times of peace could lead to devastating consequences in times of war."

Lady Linzy nodded her approval, a slight smile—the first one Terea had seen on her—curving the corners of her mouth.

"We're not at war," Lord Jagur said again. "And it isn't a hasty decision. You spent hours and hours with our king drafting a treaty that met with both of your approval."

Terea nodded. "Perhaps. But I don't remember any of that."

"Right. Because you—and this nation—were attacked before you could sign. That should tell you something. Someone doesn't want this treaty to go through. Spies, using my visit as a way to sneak into the kingdom and attack the woman I love are behind this. This treaty will benefit both our nations, and someone is trying to thwart that."

He cast his gaze slowly around the table. "Whoever it is, they are making you all doubt me. Making *her* doubt me." He gestured toward Terea. "Worse, making her doubt herself."

He turned to look at Terea, his eyes pleading. "Once the treaty is signed, I can insist that the king send help. His best men to investigate, and soldiers to help rid this country of spies and those who would seek to harm you, my love."

Terea's heart warmed. He must care very deeply in order to get so animated in his desire to protect her.

She had chosen her future spouse well.

But though her heart yearned to please him, to sign the treaty that would allow him to protect her fully, he was right about one thing—she didn't trust herself.

How could she possibly reach an unbiased decision when she didn't remember the nuances of her country's political system or the reasons she had come to the agreement in the first place? When she didn't remember the king of Cadalania or any conversations with him? When she didn't understand the possible repercussions she might face if she did what he asked?

She placed a hand on his. "I'm sorry, but I cannot sign this. Not yet. I need more information. I can't make decisions for my country based on meetings I don't remember having with a man I don't know. I will need to think on it and discuss it further with Parliament after I've had a chance to consider the ramifications."

Lord Jagur pulled his hands away and placed them in his lap. His knuckles turned white as he clenched his tunic. "I understand, my love. Know that I only want what is best for both our countries, and I will do all I can to help you make the right decision."

Trust

"You look beautiful, my love," Jagur said. He touched her cheek with his fingertips, and his warm eyes betrayed the pent-up passion he felt when he looked at her.

A flush crept up Terea's cheeks. She was not used to people commenting on her looks.

Or was she?

She blinked to shove those thoughts away, but they nagged at her, oppressive, like the weight that clouded her mind.

How could she not know something so basic, like whether men were in the habit of flattering her, yet remember things like hating cucumbers or being afraid to ride a horse? The bits of memories that came to her were so random, so fragmented, she would never be able to put them all together. How could she even know what kind of person she was, when she didn't remember any of her actions?

Was she a good queen? Merciful? Or a tyrant, selfish and entitled?

Was she kind to servants, or were they so far beneath her notice that she treated them with disdain or contempt?

She took Jagur's outstretched hand. He entwined his fingers with hers, sending a warm tingle through her body, and led her down the hallway toward the dining hall. Their footsteps tapped on the marble floor, in perfect sync. The way she thought they should be as a couple who planned to marry.

Her steps faltered, suddenly out of step.

"What are you thinking about, my love? You seem a thousand miles away."

"It's nothing, really. Nothing new, anyway. I just can't help wondering if maybe Legerdemain would be better off if I were to step down from the throne. Let Parliament run the country."

"How can you say such things? You are a good and wise queen. Selfless in all things. It's why I fell in love with you."

She smiled at him. It still felt strange for him to so readily declare his love, but she was getting used to it.

His words didn't change the facts, however. "So you say. But how can I know for sure? And how can I make decisions based on hearsay?"

He paused and turned her to face him, taking her other hand in his. "My love, I know how hard this must be for you. But if you will just trust me, I will help you. We have spent countless hours in conversation about this. I know your heart in politics, as surely as in the rest of life. Your dreams, your desires, your feelings… I want to help you, but I can't do that as long as you refuse to trust me."

"I'm trying, I just…" she stopped. What could she say? She had no words to make sense of the tumbling emotions in her head, even to herself—how could she possibly explain them to him? "I'm trying," she said again.

"I'm sure you are, but I don't know how long I can go on like this. I keep seeing glimpses of the woman I knew, but you keep pushing her back, out of my reach."

Terea drew back, his words like a slap. "That's not what I'm doing."

"Isn't it? Every time I start to get close to you, you pull away, and even the memories of us you do have, like writing long love letters, fade. The Healer says you're in good health physically, so what else can it be, other than you trying to find a reason to keep from moving forward. Do you want to break off our engagement?"

Tears stung Terea's eyes. "I'm sorry. I didn't mean to make you feel that way. I do… want to remember what we had. I want to love you like I did. I don't want to break our engagement, truly I don't."

She pulled him into an embrace, to emphasize the truth of her words.

He patted her back, but the warmth was gone from his touch.

She held him tighter. She couldn't lose him. He was the strongest connection she had to who she was before. Even her mother and Arna were of little help in uncovering her deepest thoughts and feelings. If she was to believe the letters written by her own hand—and she had to, or what else did she have?—he was the only one who really knew her.

Was he right? Was she intentionally putting distance between them without even realizing it? Was she so afraid to remember that she intentionally kept him at arm's length? She had to get back to herself, had to reclaim her memories, her life. And opening herself to Jagur was the best way to do that.

"I do trust you," she said, as much to convince herself as him. "Tomorrow, I am supposed to read petitions and tax regulations. Will you help me? Will you show me what I would've done before? How I would've seen things?"

Jagur smiled and kissed her cheek. "There's my love. I knew you were in there. I would be happy to help."

He held her hand again, his touch tender and loving as he led continued down the hallway to the dining hall.

"I'm told there is to be an acrobatic performance after dinner," he said. "You always did love a good acrobat."

Terea smiled at him. She didn't remember loving acrobats, but she didn't remember not loving them, either, and if her betrothed said it was so, it must be.

Control

Felyp crouched in the rafters in the queen's private chambers.

The queen seemed worse today. Some days her mind seemed functional. She asked questions, made decisions, gave instructions. But other days, like today, she seemed almost childlike in her innocence and inability.

Her maid helped her with the smallest of tasks, from brushing her hair to choosing her breakfast. These relapses always seemed to happen after some sort of major event. Yesterday, there had been a Council meeting. He still had not found a way to listen in on those—no trapdoor in the rafters opened into the Council room. But he'd followed Lord Jagur afterward.

Lord Jagur met with a woman, but Felyp wasn't sure who. The woman obscured herself with magic every time they met. It seemed odd, because Felyp felt certain Lord Jagur knew the woman's identity, yet he didn't give any details away. Perhaps the magical woman knew she was in danger of being watched. Perhaps she was just paranoid. But every time the two met to discuss their plans, the woman remained hidden and unidentifiable. He still had not figured out who she was.

She hated the queen, though. Resented her. The resentment went back to the previous king—something about his rule had embittered the magical woman, and she was now using Jagur and the queen to achieve her own ends.

And the queen had no idea. Felyp looked down at where the queen sat, her needle rhythmically going in and out of a truly terrible embroidered lilac. Lord Jagur sat next to her, reading reports from Cadalania.

Jagur grunted.

"What is it?" Queen Terea asked.

"Oh, nothing you need to concern yourself with," Lord Jagur said.

"Please, I would like to know."

Lord Jagur sighed, as though her request personally aggrieved him. "The king is feeling pressure from Sunnland to increase trade routes and expand imports from surrounding nations. He is organizing his army to march on Sunnland and push them back from their borders. I'm going to suggest to the Council that we help."

"But Legerdemain has always been politically neutral," Queen Terea said.

"Yes, and look what has happened. Legerdemain is a tiny nation, backwards in technology, reliant on agriculture and mining, and with the same borders it has had for five hundred years."

"What is wrong with that?" The queen sounded genuinely confused. "We are a happy land, our people content. We work hard and we enjoy our lives. People are free to live their lives, run their businesses, travel— whatever they wish. Why should we need to expand or change?"

"Leave the strategizing to me, my love. You cannot hope to understand the nuances of leadership and growth in your current condition."

Felyp considered the man's words. Every time he spoke, he contradicted himself, yet the queen never doubted him, never seemed to see what was happening. One moment he was assuring her of his love, commending her on her wisdom and ability to rule, and the next he undermined her every thought. No wonder the queen didn't know her own mind, with so many disparate thoughts weaving back and forth.

But why did she listen to him? Could she not see the way he was changing his words and actions to fit his mood, to get her to believe whatever he told her? Why did she not see through that? Why did she not confront him on his double meanings and manipulations?

The queen took a sip of her tea and nodded. "Of course, you are right. I trust you."

Felyp groaned inwardly. The queen was a simple-minded fool. The General had spoken so highly of her—but this woman was a shell, a puppet. Why had the General fixed his sights on this woman, of all? The ruler of a tiny nation, a happy, content little place, with no desire to grow or expand. How had the General concluded this was someone worthy of rule? Worthy of his attention?

That would be the first thing Felyp would ask, when he finally found him.

But how would he find the General? How would he fix this? The General had not left any messages, any clue as to his whereabouts. But he wasn't dead. The spell that connected Felyp to the General had not been severed. If it had, there would have been an explosion, of sorts, a shattering of artifacts within the palace, and a spell on the person who killed him. A disease that would spread from his murderer outward to the people he loved, until everyone was ill or the murderer was executed.

Felyp felt uncomfortable with the magic spell, but the General had assured him it was for the best, and he trusted the General. More than he trusted himself.

The General had a plan. And the plan involved Queen Terea. And it was Felyp's duty to see the plan to fruition, as long as the General was alive.

That meant protecting the queen, even if she was too simple to understand what was going on.

One thing he knew, though—Jagur could not be trusted. Jagur controlled the queen for his own purposes, but how, Felyp had not yet discovered.

"Jagur," the queen began, her voice tentative, "how will helping Cadalania help us?"

"What do you mean?" Jagur asked.

"What business is it of ours whether Cadalania and Sunnland share borders or wipe each other out? Our trade routes remain, and if they

58

don't, then we will create new ones when the time comes. Our gemstones are renowned across the continent. As long as we continue to provide them, we'll never lack for trade or supplies. It is not our duty to maintain peace for any nation but our own."

Lord Jagur motioned to the maid, who hurried over and refilled the queen's tea.

"I'll explain later, when we are in Council. Remember, I am doing everything to help you and see you and your nation prosper. Trust me, my love."

The queen sipped her tea. "I do trust you. You know I do."

Her voice sounded further away, more distant and manufactured than before.

The tea. The tea and Jagur's voice. There must be some sort of spell he was using to make his words have power over her. Every time he called her "my love," she complied without hesitation. And the tea seemed to weaken her mind.

How had he not seen it before? How had he not recognized it? The queen was not weak, she was under a spell.

Jagur wasn't just manipulating her, he owned her. He would take her kingdom, and she would have no idea. And if he did that, it would be nearly impossible for the General to take it back.

Somehow, he needed to find the General and help the queen before Lord Jagur got her kingdom away from her completely.

Threads

Something crinkled when Terea moved her head on her pillow. She groaned at the sliver of light that came through the window and landed on her face. That didn't usually happen. Arna didn't usually open the drapes until she was awake.

She sat up and blinked, and realized the light had only been bright because it landed directly on her face, but it still held the pale glow of early morning.

"Arna?" she called out softly.

No answer. Her maid must still be asleep in the next room.

She tried to think back to the evening before.

It was so hard to think, especially first thing in the morning, before her mind had a chance to clear from her sleep. She could still taste the tea they gave her to help her rest, lingering in the back of her throat.

She took a sip of water from the glass on her bedside table and forced her mind back to the previous evening.

Arna had closed the blinds all the way. She was certain of it. There was a draft, even though the windows were shuttered tightly. The winter chill that seeped through even the slightest crack. Arna had made sure the heavy curtains blocked out the cold.

So who had opened them? Perhaps Arna had come in the night to check on her, and had adjusted them, not realizing she'd left a gap.

Yes, that must be it.

She lay back. There was still time to sleep before she must arise and attend to her duties.

The pillow crinkled again. Yes, that was what had awakened her the first time. What was that?

She reached under the pillow in search of the sound, and her hand brushed some sort of parchment.

She pulled it out. It was a small piece of parchment, folded over itself. Her name was scrawled across the outside in handwriting she didn't recognize. Who had put that there? It wasn't there the night before. She would have noticed if she'd tried to fall asleep and her pillow crinkled. Could it have been left by whomever opened the drapes?

The idea that someone could sneak into her room and leave something for her without Arna or any of her guards knowing filled her with a sickening horror.

She should call Jagur in at once. He would know what to do. And he would want to know if someone was stalking her in the night.

But whoever it was hadn't tried to harm her. He—or she—had the opportunity to kill her in her sleep and no one would've been the wiser. It wasn't an assassination, and all they had done was open her drapes and left her a note.

The drapes must have been on purpose. The intruder had intended for her to wake up and find the note before Arna or anyone else came in to check on her that morning.

She opened it slowly and looked at the words, trying to make sense of them.

Majesty. Everything you have been told is a lie. Those who say they love you are trying to harm you. Trust no one. I am seeking proof, but this I know—their lies hang by threads. Pull one, and the whole scheme will unravel.

There was no signature, no indication whatsoever to give a clue who might have placed the note under her pillow.

Someone who had access to her rooms. Someone who knew more than she did.

But what threads did he mean? What lies?

Who loved her that might want to harm her?

The only people who loved her were her mother and Jagur. Maybe Sir Cristofer, or the other members of Parliament. Parliament could be lying to her. They were trying to stop the treaty from going forward, trying to stop her from allying Legerdemain with her neighbors. Were they who the note was talking about? Was that one of the threads they wanted her to pull?

They must be. She had to find out more about the treaty. Had to find out why they were trying so hard to stop it.

But what if that wasn't the lie? What if that wasn't the thread? What if someone else was lying to her?

Or—and she couldn't believe this wasn't her first thought—what if the writer of the note was the one lying? Trying to create suspicion when there was nothing to be worried about? If someone wanted to undermine her rule, what better way than to create doubt and make her suspicious of the people she trusted most?

That was a genius plan, and far more plausible than the people who she trusted, who she had trusted before she lost her memory, turning against her and lying to her.

Besides, whoever had planted the note had not even been forward enough to tell her himself. He snuck into her room at night and planted an anonymous note. She couldn't possibly trust someone like that.

Whoever planted the note was her enemy. When she found him, she would unravel the lies that he claimed were going to harm her.

She heard motion coming from the other room—Arna's room.

Her heart thudded against her chest. She scrambled out of bed and tossed the parchment into the fire.

She stopped to stare at it. Why? Why had that been her first instinct? What would it matter if Arna knew about the note? In fact, she should tell Arna—Jagur, too. They needed to know if someone had accessed her in the middle of the night. They needed to know there was a threat to her security.

Yet some instinct had told her to hide the evidence, to keep the information about the intruder to herself.

He was the enemy, of that she was absolutely certain. But just in case...

She needed to start pulling threads. She needed to see what—if anything—would unravel when she did.

The door opened and Arna paused in the doorway. "Good morning, Majesty. You're up early. Are you well?"

Terea nodded. "Just a little chilled."

"I'll bank the fire," Arna said. She tilted her head to one side. "Are you certain you're feeling all right? Perhaps you should go back to bed for a bit."

Terea shook her head. "I'm fine, really. I can't go back to bed. I have a meeting with Parliament today."

Arna nodded. "Very well. I'll get the fire going and then I'll get your breakfast and your tea."

Terea watched her while she worked. Arna was faithful. Trustworthy. A friend.

Arna would never betray her.

But suddenly, she wasn't sure. How did she know who she could really trust?

Doubt

"I just don't understand how the treaty benefits Legerdemain," Terea said.

She and Jagur sat at the table in her chambers, drinking tea and talking. What had started out as a romantic interlude, talking about their future and making plans, had quickly devolved into a political discussion.

Legerdemainian law had no gender distinctions for inheriting the throne. The oldest child inherited the throne, regardless of gender, and the royal line was passed down from oldest child to oldest child in every generation, unless a death or something else subverted the line of succession.

Jagur had said that such narrow thinking would be something Legerdemainians would learn to overcome when they sent nobles to Cadalania for education, after the treaty was signed.

"It seems as though all the concessions are on Legerdemain, and all the rewards on Cadalania," Terea said. "Why would I have agreed to this?"

"Because it's about more than crops," Jagur said. "It's about education and protection. Legerdemain is small. Easy to overwhelm."

"We've been independent and politically neutral for six hundred years. Why would we need protection now? Especially if it means promising that our sorcerers and even base magic users, like midwives, must fight on the side of Cadalania?"

"It's a protection for both of us. Cadalania sits between Legerdemain and all the nations to the south and east. If we are overrun, so are you. A pledge to help us is a defense for yourself, my love."

Terea rubbed her head. The way he said it sounded so logical, so common sense.

But if it was so good for everyone, why did she have doubts? Why did Parliament?

"Won't we be more vulnerable to attack, once the world finds out we're no longer neutral?"

"It won't change anything about the way other nations see you. You're still tucked in this little pocket of country, between mountains and forest. All it does is make us both stronger, because we have someone to rely on."

A memory wound its way into Terea's mind. She sat with a man whose face she couldn't quite see. Something warm filled her from her toes to her fingertips, so intense she thought her heart might burst.

What was this? Who was the man, and why did she fee like he was everything?

We all need someone we can rely on, he'd said.

"My love?" Jagur's voice snapped her out of her memory.

She looked at him. "You're right. I... I'll consider it."

He squeezed her hand. "I knew you would see that it's the right thing. Come, my love. Let us walk."

Terea followed him out to the garden. He chatted about small things, like the letter he'd gotten from his brother and how much he enjoyed their northern recipes, and how he couldn't wait to begin planning their wedding. Terea smiled and agreed with him, but her thoughts kept returning to her memory. Who was the man? And what did it mean?

Cold wind swept down from around the castle's battlements.

Terea inhaled. "It will snow tonight."

"How can you tell?" Jagur asked.

"I don't know. I just know it will."

He patted her arm. "Just don't put too much stock in your feelings. They aren't reliable."

Another gust of wind whipped Terea's cloak around her. "We should get inside. It's almost dinner time." She unlinked her arm and hurried across the garden to the door where Arna, her ever-present shadow, waited.

"Are you quite all right, Majesty?" Arna asked.

Terea nodded. "I think so. But something happened."

She waited until they were closed in her room to speak. "I remembered something."

Arna gasped, and a smile stretched her features. "That's wonderful, Majesty! What was it? Something about Lord Jagur?"

Terea shook her head. "Not him. A man. I don't know who he was, but I loved him. Trusted him. I think he wants me to sign the treaty."

"A man you love? But not Jagur?"

Terea shook her head. "I don't think so. He seemed completely familiar to me, in a way that Jagur doesn't. Did I ever love anyone else?"

"Not that I know of, Majesty, and I have not left your side in nearly three years. But perhaps he is a product of your own mind? A part of you that you can't remember, but that is trying to tell you what you should do?"

Terea frowned. Would she love someone that deeply if she had made him up inside her own head? It didn't make sense. Nothing made sense. Why couldn't she just remember? What was wrong with her?

The weight of her own inability to function pressed on her, as heavy as the cloud that seemed to cover her every action, obscuring her thoughts, making her feel like she was wading through a swamp with every step.

That memory, though. That voice.

It was so clear, so... *true.*

She couldn't have imagined it. She couldn't have made that up. It was the most real thing in her life.

The man had to be real. But if he was, where was he? Why did Arna not remember him?

And why did she feel like she loved him, when she knew, by her own hand, that she loved Jagur?

"I think perhaps I'll skip dinner tonight," she said. She needed time to sort through her own thoughts and feelings, without the pressure of an audience or anyone else's voices speaking into her head.

"Majesty, if I may be so bold... everyone already expects you to fail. They think you are broken. If you want them to know you are still worth of your crown, you have to appear before them. Show them you know your own mind, and that you can make decisions for yourself."

Terea nodded, resigned to the knowledge that Arna was right. She allowed Arna to help her dress for dinner, and marched boldly to the dining hall to do her duty to her country, but the nagging thought still lingered... was she capable of being the queen?

Lost Love

Arna glanced both directions along the hallway to ensure no one saw her before she rapped lightly on the door.

Though no one would question her presence in any part of the palace, her contact had insisted it was best not to be seen together.

The door opened and Arna slipped inside.

Her contact sat at a table, a sliver of sunlight from a gap in the drapes casting a blinding glare through the window between Arna and her contact, leaving the contact shrouded so Arna could not see her face.

At least, Arna thought it was a she.

The contact used magic to obscure her features and voice.

A small, round table covered with a red cloth sat between them, a bowl of water and a jar of herbs placed atop it.

"You have news?" the contact asked.

"Yes. The queen…" She stopped, her hands twisting together in painful wringing. "I want to see my daughter."

"Your daughter is fine and will continue to be so unless you fail. The queen?"

Arna swallowed the emotion that rose up in her throat. "She had a memory this morning. Of the invasion. She says she remembers feeling betrayed, and sad. She couldn't remember any specifics, but she knows someone she trusted betrayed her."

"That's good. We can work with that. Anything else?"

Arna nodded. "Yesterday, she remembered a face. A man, but not Lord Jagur. But she said he was someone she loved."

"We can make her forget him."

"I'm not sure we can," Arna said. "The memory came when she was asking about the treaty with Cadalania. She was unwilling to sign, but when she remembered the man, it was like she also remembered that he wanted her to sign. Whoever he is, she trusts him. More than she even trusts me."

"We can convince her to sign," the contact insisted. "With or without the memory."

"It might not matter. Since she has been so reluctant, Parliament has become wary. If she suddenly becomes an advocate, they may overrule her."

"So we have to find a way to convince Parliament that the treaty needs to be signed, as well," the contact said.

Arna didn't answer. She didn't think she was supposed to.

"Is there any way you can convince her the memory she had actually was of Jagur?"

"I don't know. I can try. And I could try to find out who he actually is. Or was."

"No, I don't want her digging around those memories. Better to let her think she's confused on the details. Has she given any indication that she loves Jagur? Trusts him?"

"He is gaining her trust. I think she is beginning to have feelings for him, but it is hard to determine how deep those go."

The contact nodded. "Keep encouraging that."

Arna nodded. "I will. But... my daughter?"

The contact sighed and sprinkled the herbs into the bowl on the table. A vision formed, revealing a grassy field with a forest beyond. Arna's daughter ran, chasing a butterfly and giggling.

Arna's heart swelled. She reached out a hand, as though she could touch the soft, round cheeks or hug the plump, cherubic body to her through the vision.

Her fingertips touched the cool water and the vision faded.

"Not long now," the contact said. "Once the queen signs the treaty, you will be back with your daughter."

Arna sniffed. "I will see to it." She stepped carefully out into the hallway, then hurried to the courtyard where Terea walked with Jagur, her arm linked in his and his hand atop hers, and fell into step behind them.

"Tell me about when we first met," Terea said. "Did we like each other immediately, or did we have to get to know one another first?"

Arna followed few paces behind them, close enough to be on hand if she was needed, but far enough that she wouldn't be obtrusive.

Jagur chuckled. "It was at the Cadalanian capitol. You were there as an ambassador, to inspect the standing of the current trade agreements and to discuss the possibility of expanding the parameters. We met in the hallway, outside the king's council hall. I made a joke about how the treaty would expire before we were called in to discuss it."

Terea stopped, her eyes searching Jagur's face. "I remember that. I remember thinking I wouldn't mind sitting in that hallway indefinitely if it meant sitting in such attractive company. But... I don't remember you. I remember... I don't know for sure."

Jagur looked hurt. "Of course it was me. The only other people in the hallway were Arna and one of the king's guards."

Arna stepped forward. "It's true, Majesty. You stared at Lord Jagur so long it even made me blush. Later, you commented on how distinguished his beard looked."

Terea blinked slowly. "Yes... yes, of course you're right. It was you."

Jagur smiled and patted her hand.

"I'm sorry," Terea said. "I don't mean to keep confusing things."

"I know you're trying," Jagur said.

Arna quickly nodded agreement. "The Healer said sometimes that might happen. The pictures in your head might get jumbled as your mind is trying to make sense of the fragments of memory, making you think you saw something you didn't."

"I suppose that must be it," Terea said. She smiled at Jagur. "I am trying. I don't mean to be insensitive."

"It's all right, my love," Jagur said. "I am just holding on to the hope that somewhere deep inside, you remember that you love me."

The General

"A word, Majesty?"

Terea turned to see a man in his middle years with dark hair and eyes and a few days' growth on his chin, standing in the shadow of an empty servants' passageway. She thought maybe it went to the kitchens, but she wasn't sure, and no candles or torches lit the walls or gave any indication of the direction it went.

The man wrung a cloth cap between gnarled fingers and shifted from one foot to the other.

Terea glanced up and down the hallway she'd been walking, but there was no one else around. Arna had gone to fetch some tea, and Jagur was meeting with his retinue. Her heart sped up a little. She shouldn't feel threatened in her own castle, but after everything that had happened…

"Please, Majesty. I have important information for you. But I had to wait until you were alone."

Terea gulped. "Do I know you?"

"No, Majesty."

She exhaled slightly. It was worse to not recognize someone she should know. Somehow, the fact that he was a stranger made him easier to talk to. Still, she couldn't afford to be flippant. "Why should I trust you?"

He shook his head, his eyes taking on a sad cast. "I have no reason to expect that you would, Majesty. I only have to try."

"Who asked you?"

"The General, Majesty."

The General.

Something about that name quickened everything in her, sending her heart racing and making her fingers and toes tingle. Who was the General?

She had no idea. She couldn't tell why she knew that name, or why it was important, but she knew it was. Something deep inside her gut told her she could trust whatever the General said.

"What is it?" she asked.

The man visibly relaxed, his eyes widening in a hopeful look as he gazed into hers. "He said to tell you... before the invasion, he told me that if anything happened to him, I should tell you that the spy network goes deeper than he imagined. Cadalania's enemies are your enemies, but things are not as they seem."

Terea inhaled. So Jagur was right—they had a shared enemy. She should have trusted he was only trying to help.

The man twisted the cap between his fingers again. "The General also said to wait for him—he will return, but do not trust anyone until he does. The invasion was not solely to try to take your throne—there is something much worse in play, and you must not trust anyone."

The invasion was not intended to take her throne? The Council seemed convinced, based on the interrogations they'd done of the spies they'd found, that the spies had used Jagur's retinue to sneak into the palace and kill her. A Cadalaian as the puppetmaster, with a distant cousin placed upon the throne. Jagur and his men had saved her life— though not her memory.

The spies were being ferreted out and imprisoned. Jagur had told her that was so. The Council believed they had stopped the imminent threat, and things could move on as planned.

But the General said otherwise.

The General... but she didn't know the General. She had no reason to trust him, and every reason to trust Jagur.

"Where is the General now?" she asked.

The man shook his head. "I do not know, Majesty. I have spent the last couple of weeks trying to get you alone. I have not seen him since before the invasion."

Panic she couldn't explain clutched Terea's heart. "Are you certain he's alive?"

"Yes, Majesty. I would know if he were dead, and so would you. He promised he would return, and he will."

"How? How would I know?"

The man shrugged. "Magic."

Despite the sick feeling in her stomach, the man's words rang true. The General was not dead. He was alive somewhere, and he had promised to return. She only needed to wait. She just needed to trust him.

But how could she? How could she possibly trust him when she had no idea who he was?

Yet despite all reason, she did trust him. And she trusted the man he had sent.

"What is your name?" she asked.

"Felyp, Majesty."

"You will be honored as my guest, Felyp," Terea said. "Come, we will get you cleaned and fed."

Felyp shrank deeper into the shadows. "With all due respect, Majesty, I cannot. My connection to the General makes me a target. If I am found, I will be imprisoned for espionage. I must continue with the work the General entrusted to me. I will make you aware if I come across any new information."

"What work is that?"

"I must find the person at the heart of this threat against you. I have those I suspect, but I cannot prove it yet. I must also find the General. Fear not, Majesty. All will be well."

"How will I find you?"

"You won't. I'll find you. Pull the threads, Majesty. Unravel the truth." With that, Felyp shrank back into the hallway and disappeared into the shadows.

Terea gasped. The threads. That was familiar—someone had tried to warn her before. She'd heard that very phrase, but now she couldn't remember where.

She tried to follow Felyp, but he was already gone.

Who was he? And who was the General? And why did she suddenly feel more vulnerable than ever?

Arna rounded the corner, a cup in her hand. "There you are, Majesty. I've brought your tea."

Compliance

"What do you mean she's refusing to sign?"

Arna cringed at the cold, harsh anger evident in the magical woman's tone.

"You told me she believed you. That she believed the man in her memory was Jagur, and that she was supposed to sign the treaty."

"She did. She was ready to sign. Something happened, but she won't tell me what."

"Did she see anyone? Speak to anyone? You're supposed to be with her at all times."

"I have been!" Arna insisted. "I never leave her side, except to get her more tea or to fetch the Healer or Jagur for her. Never more than moments from her side. Never long enough for her to have a secret meeting. She has never seen anyone that has not been monitored, and she has never had an opportunity to make plans that we don't know about."

"Then how? How could this happen?"

"I don't know. I think the tea is losing its efficacy."

"The Healer has assured me that can't happen."

Arna lifted her hands in a gesture of helplessness. "You know how stubborn and strong-willed the queen is. She's fighting it."

"How is that possible?"

"I have no idea. I don't know magic. I'm only doing what I'm told."

The magical woman sighed, her breath coming out in a long, angry puff. "I need the treaty signed, and I need it signed *now*. Tell the Healer to do whatever is necessary to force compliance. I don't have time to keep waiting for the queen to come around or for Jagur to work his charms on her. And remember, if you fail me, you fail your daughter."

Arna choked back tears and curtsied. "I won't fail you."

She hurried from the room. The queen was with Jagur, so she was safe for now, so Arna made her way to the Healer's chambers. She relayed the magical woman's message.

The Healer sighed, frustration crossing her features. "I cannot make the queen compliant *and* give her enough of her own mind to be believable. Why do I have to keep explaining this?"

"The sorceress seemed uninterested in making Terea's role believable. She said whatever is necessary to force her to sign the treaty."

"The queen is strong. I've never seen anyone fight so hard against this kind of spell. Usually, they take what memories they are given and create the fabricated reality that I tell them to. It is much easier on the mind to submit to the spell, and she has been fighting it from the beginning. It will take a significant amount of magic to force this."

"Whatever is necessary," Arna said.

The Healer handed Arna a small pouch of dried herbs. "Take the queen her tea, and sprinkle this on her dinner. This will soften her mind and make her more susceptible. I will meet you in the queen's sitting room after dinner to do the spell."

She sprinkled a different herb into a cup of water and handed it to Arna. "Drink this. It will act as an antidote for the spell that I will do, so you don't accidentally get influenced as well."

Arna looked at the cup. She didn't trust the Healer, but what choice did she have? She had no doubt that the sorceress would do exactly what she'd threatened, torturing and killing Arna's daughter to force her to do as she was told.

She drank.

Obediently, she forced the queen to drink her tea, and sprinkled the herbs on the queen's food. Terea already seemed dazed and childlike as Arna walked her back to her room after dinner.

"Have a seat, Majesty. The Healer will be coming soon to check on you."

"Yes. Good. Thank you," the queen said, her words slurring together almost drunkenly.

The Healer arrived a few moments later. "Good evening, your Majesty. You're looking well. How are you feeling?"

The queen looked up, her eyes glazed. "I am well, thank you."

"Good, good. I'm very pleased with your progress. I'm just going to check a few things."

The Healer tossed some herbs into the fire, creating a sickly sweet smoke that filled the room. Was this what she'd given Arna the herbs to combat?

The smoke made her feel tired, woozy—unable to think clearly. Was this how the queen felt all the time?

The Healer took a gemstone from her pouch—a ruby, Arna thought—and closed her eyes. Arna couldn't see or feel the energy that she knew must be pulsing through the gem, but she could see the strain it put on the Healer to use it.

The Healer spoke in a lilting, sing-song tone. "Terea, your kingdom needs you. You must sign the treaty. Lord Jagur knows what is best. You love him. You must listen to what he tells you. He will guide you. Obey Lord Jagur. Sign the treaty."

"I can't. It is not good for Legerdemain."

"You're wrong," the Healer said. "Listen to my voice. You know my voice. You trust my voice. You must sign the treaty."

"I... mustn't. The threads... I have to pull the threads."

Arna canted her head to the side. What threads? What was she talking about?

"Listen to my voice. Obey my voice. Obey Jagur's voice. You are his love. He knows what's best. You will sign the treaty."

The queen protested again, and again the Healer repeated her words.

Arna blinked, fighting the drowsy feeling that tried to overwhelm her. How much worse would this have been if the Healer hadn't given her the antidote earlier?

She had to keep her mind sharp. She stepped out into the hallway and took a deep breath of clean air. The fog started to lift. She squeezed back tears. What the Healer—and Jagur and the sorceress, whoever she was—were doing was very, very wrong. She hated to be part of it, yet what choice did she have? Her daughter's life was at stake.

She took another deep breath and went back into the queen's room.

The queen's protests were more slurred, less coherent, less vehement already. But the Healer looked ready to collapse. Could she go on much longer?

Arna took the Healer a glass of water, which she took with a smile. After a long gulp, she continued her spell.

After a few more rounds, the queen finally succumbed to the spell.

"I will sign the treaty," she said, in a slow, drawling voice.

"You will sign the treaty. Good," the Healer said. Her hand went limp and the ruby clattered to the floor. She looked at Arna. "Get her to bed, and then fetch me something to eat."

Arna nodded and hurried to obey. She always obeyed. She had no other choice.

Waiting

"I am so pleased you have finally seen the truth, my love," Jagur smiled.

The pen in Terea's hand hovered over the treaty. She had been so certain earlier. This was the best thing for her country. Jagur had explained it. And she'd had that memory, wherein the person she trusted said… what had he said?

She knew… It was important. He wanted her to sign. At least… she thought he did.

The man in the memory… who was he? Oh, yes, he was Jagur, wasn't he?

Yes, it had to be him. That's what he said. Of course it was him.

She loved him. Trusted him. And he wanted her to sign. Because he loved her and wanted the best for their countries.

"That's it, my love. Just there."

She lowered the pen and started to sign, but the ink was dry.

She dipped it again, then before her cloudy mind could confuse her again, scrawled her name on the line, then again on the second copy, the one Jagur would send to Cadalania for their records.

Jagur snatched up the treaty. "Very good, my love. I will send this immediately, and with it, a request for men who can investigate the spies and claims of a usurper."

Terea nodded and took a sip of her tea. Weariness overwhelmed her. All she wanted was to take a long rest.

"And now, my love, I think we should discuss our wedding. We've been putting it off long enough. I was hoping you would be fully well, but… I just don't want to wait any longer to make you my bride." He smiled, love filling his eyes. "And I know you feel the same about me."

Terea's throat tightened. She understood—how long had they been betrothed? A year? And all the time she'd been ill, since the attack, he'd been so patient with her, so tender and loving, waiting for her to remember him, to love him as he loved her.

Yet… the thought of actually going through with it…

She took another sip of her tea to delay answering. But she couldn't delay forever. She took a deep breath and nodded slowly. "We should discuss it."

She just thought before she actually married him, she'd remember… *anything*. She thought she'd love him.

But she couldn't make him wait forever. It wasn't fair to him. He trusted in the depth of their love—why couldn't she? He didn't seem to mind that her memory hadn't fully returned, so perhaps she should trust him more. Maybe if she fully gave herself to him, whatever pieces of her mind were still fighting to stay in the shadows would finally be free.

But she was supposed to wait. A man had come to her, told her to wait. What man? Who was he? Why couldn't she remember? He'd said someone would return… but who? She was supposed to wait for him… or was she? Was that a real memory? Or was it a twisted memory, like the other one, the one who was really Jagur?

Yes, that must be it. She was supposed to wait for Jagur, but he was here. He had returned. And he was waiting for her. She nodded again. "Yes. We should talk. But we should wait for the ceremony until after the investigation."

Jagur's eyes hardened and he smiled through clenched teeth. "Whatever you wish. I only want to protect you, my love. But at every turn, you push me away. All I am trying to do is help you."

"I know. And I'm sure I want that, too. But how can I focus on a wedding when there is someone trying to usurp my throne?"

81

"Of course." Jagur rose from the table. He extended an arm, but his touch was cool, distant.

Guilt washed over Terea. She'd made him angry. Hurt him. It was unfair of her. Cruel, even, to keep putting him off. What if her memories never returned? She couldn't leave him waiting forever.

She must either marry him or break their engagement.

But she couldn't break the engagement, not after all he'd done for her. All he'd given up for her. All he wanted was her love in return for countless sacrifices on his part, and this was how she treated him?

No wonder he was so upset.

She sighed and intertwined his fingers with his. "A spring wedding might be nice. I'm told there are orchards by the West Village that blossom with the most beautiful white flowers."

He pulled his hand away. "And when spring arrives, will you want to change it to summer? Or perhaps autumn, when the leaves are turning? Or perhaps we'll never get married and you'll just keep dragging me along, giving me just enough hope to keep from breaking off our betrothal, when you have no intention of following through. You'll use me to secure peaceful relations with Cadalania, and when you've gotten all you can, you'll send me home, too old and worn down with unreciprocated love to ever be able to move on with my life."

Terea stopped, her cheeks burning as though she'd been slapped.

She opened her mouth, but no words came out. What could she say? He was right.

Jagur cast one last, pained look at her before stalking away.

Terea's eyes filled. She'd used him shamelessly. There was only one way to fix it. She had to marry him, and the sooner the better.

Intimacy

"You make me so happy, my love." Jagur smiled at Terea.

She smiled back, but her insides churned. He made her happy, too. She felt sure of it. The way he cared for her and helped her, the way he did everything to benefit her… Of course she loved him as much as he loved her.

She had a vague recollection of someone else—a man she'd known a long time ago. Or had she? Everyone said Jagur was the only man she had ever loved.

So why did it feel so wrong that in the morning they'd be married? She felt sure that most brides were excited by the prospect of marrying their loves, and Jagur had assured her—she had assured herself, looking at their correspondence—that she felt the same.

The terror in the pit of her stomach telling her she was making a mistake wouldn't relent.

But what choice did she have? She'd given her word. She knew she couldn't run the country on her own, and Jagur had been nothing but helpful. Especially with her mind in as fragile a state as it was, she needed him.

She couldn't disappoint him, not after all he'd done. Her own misgivings were due to her illness. Her faulty memory tricked her into thinking things that weren't true. She couldn't trust herself, so she didn't trust anyone, and that wasn't fair. Not to her, not to the kingdom, and certainly not to Jagur who had sacrificed so much.

All these weeks, he'd waited patiently to make her his own. She'd promised him herself so long ago. She didn't remember, but he did, and it certainly was not fair of her to go back on her word. Especially when it made so much sense to go through with it.

Her mother had assured her that all brides felt some amount of nervousness. She herself had been sent as a bride without ever having met her future husband. Queens marrying someone they loved was virtually unheard of—Terea should be grateful that she was allowed the privilege of knowing and loving her husband. Love was usually reserved for peasants and those who with nothing to lose.

Jagur would take care of her, and he would take care of her kingdom. There was no reason to doubt him, despite the way her stomach seemed to want to flip inside-out at the thought of it.

"You seem upset," Jagur interrupted her thoughts.

"No, of course not. I am only anticipating such a large change in my life."

"It will not be such a big change," Jagur smiled. "After all, we already spend every waking moment together. It will only expand our time to the night, as well."

The way he said it sounded as though he intended the prospect to be alluring, enticing, but horror was the only emotion that Terea could feel. She hadn't even considered that part of it. She didn't want to deny him, but she felt none of the eagerness at the prospect of intimacy that she thought she ought to.

Had she ever felt that way about someone? Perhaps there was something wrong with her.

She closed her eyes and tried to remember whether or not she'd ever loved someone in that way.

A memory came to her, a man with a beard. She'd seen him before. Another memory. She loved him. They sat together on a chaise in a palace she didn't recognize, laughing over something—maybe nothing, just laughing together.

He kissed her, and she kissed him back. His fingers stroked her cheek, tangled in her hair, and he pulled her close. She wanted nothing more in that moment but to be in his arms forever.

"What are you thinking about, my love?"

"I was remembering something. Kissing."

Jagur smiled. I have been reluctant to kiss you like I used to. You have been so fragile. But I am glad the thought of our intimacy brings a smile to your face."

Terea touched her lips. She hadn't realized it, but she had been smiling.

Jagur stood and leaned over her. He brought his face to hers, touched her lips with his own. His oiled beard tickled her face, and his breath mingled with hers. His beard felt different than it had in her memory— or did it?

The memory shifted. Like the one before, when she thought it was someone else, but it wasn't, it was Jagur. His kiss sealed it, the way his lips and beard felt against her skin, the way his breath mingled with hers…

So she had loved him, wanted to be with him.

How could she have doubted such a thing?

Her own memories worked against her, but the truth stared her in the face. She and Jagur loved each other, and she wanted to be with him. She had always wanted him, and only him. And the next day, it would be finalized.

Something inside her assured her that once she was married, stable, happy, everything else would fall into place. Her memories, her kingdom, her life—it all hinged on this one act. Everything she'd done since waking up after her injury had been leading her to this one moment.

She would marry Jagur, and she would love him forever, just as he would love her. They would rule together in peace and happiness all their lives.

How could she have ever doubted it?

King

Bells chimed, ringing from the parapets where Terea and Jagur stood, hand in hand, looking out over the people who had come to wish them well.

The day was beautiful—a fresh layer of snow covered the kingdom. The mountains to the north disappeared into a heavy layer of clouds, but directly overhead, the sky was a cold, crisp blue.

Jagur smiled at Terea, and she smiled back, but a heavy weight settled in her chest. Her wedding day should have been the happiest of her life—so why did she feel such foreboding?

Was it anticipation about the night ahead? She couldn't remember if she'd ever been with a man. The idea of it filled her with anticipation, in an abstract sense, but when she looked at Jagur, handsome though he was, a strange sort of fear rose in her throat.

Jagur raised his hand to wave at the crowd of well-wishers on the ground. Terea followed his lead, smiling and waving as her people cheered her good fortune.

She looked again at her husband. Her *husband*. Why did that word not feel as joyous as she thought it should?

"It was a lovely ceremony," her mother said from behind her, joining them on the parapet, and in waving and smiling at the people. "It reminds me of my own wedding. It was a little frightening, of course. I was sent here as a peace offering."

She wrapped her cloak tighter around herself and continued. "Kirland and Legerdemain had been at odds for a couple generations, after the forest changed the nature of trade negotiations between our nations. My father, brother of the king, thought a marital alliance would help ease tensions. It worked, of course. My father was very wise in diplomacy. He really should've been king."

She sighed. "Kirland has not yet attained her rightful place as an equal power to Sunnland, but she is growing stronger. But today isn't about me. Look at you two! Such a beautiful couple."

She patted Terea's cheek. "Marriage suits you, my dear. I suppose you'll be wanting to take a marriage trip? Although not until spring, I'm sure. Traveling in this weather is hardly ideal. You should plan to visit Kirland, at any rate. Give my regards to my cousin, who now sits on the throne."

She prattled on, and Jagur gave her an indulgent smile before wrapping his arm around Terea's shoulder. "I should get my bride out of this cold," he said.

A chill ran up Terea's spine, though whether from the wind that gusted across the parapet or from the way Jagur said "my bride," she wasn't sure.

She allowed him to lead her inside and down to the great hall, where Sir Cristofer waited for them.

He'd performed the ceremony, despite his eyes saying he disapproved. All that was left was the signing of the papers before Parliament, legalizing Jagur's role as king.

The Legerdemainian royal line would run through her, but if she should die or become incapacitated without an heir, the kingdom would fall to him.

"Your Majesty, a word, before you sign, if I may?" Sir Cristofer said.

Terea unlinked her arm from Jagur's and followed Sir Cristofer to the side of the room.

"Majesty, I just want to say... it's not too late to have this marriage annulled. You have not been well, and no one will blame you if you decide it best to wait to consummate your marriage for awhile."

Terea breathed deeply. She knew Jagur would be angry, but perhaps it would be worth enduring his anger if she didn't have to go through with it right now. Sir Cristofer's kind old eyes told her he would support her decision.

Jagur could wait a little longer. Unless he left her completely—if she broke it off now, she might never get him back, and that thought terrified her more than the thought of being married to him.

But how could she be married to him when she was so uncertain of everything, including her own heart?

Sir Cristofer gave her an encouraging nod.

She turned to tell Jagur she wasn't ready to finalize their marriage and nearly toppled Arna over.

"It's time for your tea, Majesty," she said, holding out a cup that had sloshed just a little onto Arna's hands.

Tea. Yes, tea was good. It would help soothe her, help make telling Jagur a little easier. She took a sip of the warm, calming beverage, then one more, letting it fill her with its warmth.

"Come, my love," Jagur said, holding out his hand to her. "It's time to sign our marriage agreement."

"Yes, of course," Terea said. She took another sip of her tea, handed the cup to Arna, then took the pen Jagur handed her and signed the agreement, fully legalizing Jagur as her king.

Mold

The soft fuzz of mold crawled tentatively over the bits of straw in Ada's little nest. She dribbled her tea in judicious sprinkles, so as not to drown the spores.

There was enough growth now for her to feel the magical energy, but not enough yet to draw on it, even to channel it back for more growth.

Patience.

She could do nothing, so it would do no good to rush the process, and trying to force it would only risk destroying the progress she had made.

Even after all her years of living, it was a struggle to do things slowly and correctly rather than try to hurry them along.

She took one tiny vegetable—a carrot, she thought—and a few drips of the broth from the soup and placed them on the nest.

Just enough to give a hint of nourishment to her little garden.

The guard thumped down the hall and opened the grate.

"Please," Ada whispered. "I am so hungry. I cannot survive on this much longer. Isn't there anything you can do?"

"My apologies, but I've already given you tea. I can't ask for anything more."

"When will they hold my trial, then? Better to die than live through this torture forever."

The guard's eyes softened. He glanced around, as though checking for eavesdroppers, which was absurd, since he was the only one to have been in this hallway since she'd been stuck her nearly a fortnight before. "I suspect the hope is that you'll die in here without them ever having to do a thing," he muttered, just softly enough that he could deny saying anything, but not so softly that Ada's attuned ears couldn't pick it up.

"If I'm not to get a trial, will I at least be allowed to petition the queen?"

"The queen has been ill. I'm sure your trial will be scheduled when she is well," he said, louder this time.

Smart. If there were witnesses, or magical elements used for eavesdropping somewhere in the hallway, all they would catch was his compliance.

Wait, what had he said? Panic surged through her. "Ill? What do you mean, ill? What is wrong?"

"Nothing for you to worry about."

"I am the Healer. I should be by her side, to see if there's anything that can be done."

"She has a Healer attending to her. There's no need to worry."

A Healer.

That explained how they knew what to put in her tea. But who? There were other Healers in the kingdom—each of the villages had one, and the South Village had two. There were apprentices and novices and midwives and those who had some affinity for magic who had learned a little of the Healing arts here and there scattered throughout the kingdom as well, but none she could think of who would know enough to do what they had done to Ada.

"Who is the Healer? I can help her, if only you'll let me speak to her. You must believe me, the queen's wellbeing is my only priority."

"It doesn't matter what I believe. My job is to keep you fed and contained. Nothing more."

He slammed the window panel shut.

So, he believed her. Good. She could use that.

She went to her little garden and felt for the tiny, dust speck-sized fragments of magic that infused the growth. A little more. Just a little more, and then she could start to use it.

But what if it was too late? The queen was ill. A Healer was in Ada's place, doing who knew what to the queen and perhaps all of Legerdemain. The guard had given no indications as to who had imprisoned her, who had ordered her to this dungeon, who was manipulating events, or why.

A coup didn't make sense. Legerdemain was peaceful, and Parliament kept the balance of power steady. The people were prosperous, and had no reason to revolt. It had to be someone from outside their borders.

What did they want? Legerdemain was a small country, with few resources and fewer exports. It was isolated from the rest of the world by both distance and culture. What did they have that would make this little pocket worth going to all this trouble for?

Gemstones? Possibly, but if that were the goal, why would they have taken such precautions? They could've just set up robbers along the trade routes, or attacked the mines directly.

Crops? Not likely. Though the land was fertile, there was not enough to make it worth trying to take over the whole nation. Besides, she'd heard no reports of famine or drought or anything else that would make Legerdemain a temptation for food or other things.

What, then? What did Legerdemain have that other nations did not?

The realization came to her like a love spell gone wrong, pulsing through her with an oily taint.

Magic.

All over the continent, magic was limited to a favored few or banned completely. Sorcerers were few and far between, enslaved to kings or killed on sight. Only in Legerdemain was magic treated as a resource like any other. Only in Legerdemain was it taught equally to commoners and nobles alike, based on affinity and talent rather than status.

Only in Legerdemain did the balance of magic and nature exist in perfect symbiosis.

Whoever it was, whatever their ultimate goal—they had come to Legerdemain for magic. They had come not to learn and take their new knowledge back with them, they had come to steal.

The royal Legerdemainian line was keeper of powerful knowledge and artifacts, some they themselves didn't even know. If enemies of Legerdemain knew how to access those powers, they could destroy everyone in their paths, even conquer the world.

And that meant the queen was in even greater danger than Ada had realized.

She had to escape from this dungeon, and she had to do it immediately.

Invasion

"What happened during the invasion?" Terea sat at the Council room table with Sir Cristofer. Arna hovered nearby, ready to refill Terea's tea whenever she should need it.

"That is the question," Sir Cristofer said. "What we know for certain is that the night Lord Jagur arrived, someone killed several of your guards and infiltrated the castle. Servants were slaughtered mercilessly, and the nobles were hunted down. Only a few of us are still alive, and most are those of us on the Council, who were with you in the throne room, waiting to receive our guests."

"What did they want?"

"That is what we're trying to determine. The guards who were killed were those who were loyal to your father. So we know there must have been spies in place beforehand, sending out information. Those guards were men and women who knew how the country had been run for many years and who had vowed to uphold the rule of the land."

"Don't all the guards vow that?" Terea asked.

"Yes. However, the balance of power between the monarch and Parliament wavers with every generation. Your father believed in sharing power fairly equally. He believed the country was stronger if everyone's interests were represented, not just those of the royal family or the nobility. He was one of few rulers in our country who included peasants and farmers on the Council."

Terea's heart warmed. She didn't remember her father, but she admired him more with every word Sir Cristofer spoke.

"So, the invaders came in and killed those who might be a threat to the ruler. To me," Terea said.

Sir Cristofer nodded.

"Did I do this? Before my injury, could I have…"

Sir Cristofer smiled and took her hand. "I do not believe so. You followed your father in many ways. You were just coming into your rule, but you trusted Parliament and the Council, and you trusted the safeguards your father put into place."

"But if it wasn't me, who? I have no heir, no siblings. Who would benefit from destroying the Council and killing the loyal guards?"

"That is what we are still trying to determine." Sir Cristofer's gaze darted to where Arna stood. "The rumor that there is an heir somewhere have come to nothing, so the only conclusion is that foreign powers are behind this."

"I don't understand—how would killing my Council help with that? If they're going to take over by force, then wouldn't they just kill me?"

"Perhaps. But even if they kill you, they still have to control the people. Legerdemainians have a long history of freedom and self-reliance. If a foreign power came in and tried to take over, he would face a whole kingdom of angry farmers and miners. He would need a vast army in order to subdue the people, and our people would not take kindly to being controlled. More than likely, he would face a coup. However, taking out those who were loyal to your father and installing his own guards would make the transition a little smoother."

"But they did try to kill me, and failed."

"Did they? We don't know that. You were injured, but we don't know what the ultimate goal was. Perhaps it's just one phase of a greater plan. Incapacitate you so you don't know what's happening as they steal your country out from under you."

Terea swallowed. She knew what he was saying.

Jagur.

But she'd already married him. Had his plan succeeded? Was he already taking her country, without her even being aware? Had she given it to him with her marriage?

And if so, how could she stop it? Annul the marriage and send him back to Cadalania? Or, now that her memory was starting to return, perhaps she could undermine him, assert her own dominance as the ruler.

"I will help you," Sir Cristofer said.

She looked at him. Could he read her thoughts? "I don't know what to do. I don't know where to start."

"I know. And you don't know who to trust. My recommendation would be to begin by rebuilding the Council. Go out among your people and meet the merchants and farmers and miners, the leaders in your community. Find some you think are wise and knowledgeable."

Terea nodded. That seemed to be good advice.

But could she trust anyone? Even him? What if he was the one who was undermining her, trying to steal her kingdom? He was a prominent member of the Council and Parliament. He was well-respected and carried a lot of influence. He would be in a perfect position to know which guards to kill, which were loyal to her father and needed to be taken out of the way.

Was Sir Cristofer plotting against her? And how could she ever know for sure?

He smiled at her. "I understand what you must be thinking. And you shouldn't trust me, not more than you trust anyone else. I am giving you the best advice I can, but you have no reason to trust that what I'm saying is in your best interest and not my own. If you think it will help you, I will retire from Parliament so you can make your own judgments without worrying about what I am trying to do."

Terea breathed a deep sigh. On one hand, such a gesture might show that he was trustworthy, and truly trying to help. On the other, he might be gambling, trusting in her wavering, knowing that she would take his gesture as a sign of good will and using it against her to worm his way further into her trust, knowing she wouldn't take him up on the offer to retire.

Sir Cristofer smiled. "Take your time deciding, your Majesty. I am here to serve you."

"Thank you," Terea said. "I will take that into consideration. In the meantime—"

The door to the Council room burst open, cutting off her words.

Jagur stood there, a smile that seemed more like a grimace stretching across his face. "There you are, my love. You should not be meeting without me. Come, you need your rest."

Terea stood and took his extended hand.

"I hope you have not overtaxed yourself," Jagur said. He shot a glare at Arna.

"I have been making sure she has plenty of tea and is well rested," Arna said, giving him a small curtsy.

"Good." He looked at Sir Cristofer. "You are dismissed. And you would do well to maintain your distance from my wife."

Dungeon

Felyp snuck along his hiding place in the rafters, crawling along the narrow beams from the small doorway between rooms. Presumably constructed for ease of repairs, these doorways made ideal routes for getting from room to room unseen, a vital component of eavesdropping.

The queen mother gave a tongue lashing to one of the guards. "What did you give him?"

"Nothing but what you prescribed, m'lady," the guard insisted. "He gets his two meals a day."

"Then how is he ill?"

"I do not know, m'lady."

"I cannot afford for him to die. I may still need him. Get the Healer immediately."

"Yes, m'lady."

"And what of the other one?"

"Still alive, m'lady."

"How is that possible?"

"I could take more... extensive measures," the guard suggested.

The queen mother shook her head. "I do not know the extent of her powers or what safeguards she has in place. Any unnatural death could trigger a host of magical consequences. Let me know if her health changes."

The guard bowed and left the throne room.

Felyp hurried back to the doorway as quickly as he could shuffle silently.

The guard was already halfway down the long hallway from the throne room toward the main hall.

Felpy started after him, but the rafters here were too far apart to scurry quickly.

After checking to ensure no one traversed the hallway, he swung down from the rafter, his bare feet thudding softly on the stone floor. He jogged after the guard. Thus far, he'd been unable to track where the General was kept. He'd searched all the regular dungeons and some of the towers. He'd been hovering around the queen mother for several days, trying to get an idea of another place to search, and this was the first promising lead he had.

The guard wound his way down to one of the cellars in an unused part of the castle. Felyp ducked behind tapestries and into doorways and nooks, staying close enough to see where the guard went, but far enough to not be seen or noticed if the guard turned around.

At last, the guard stopped at a doorway. He gave one brief glance around before pulling the keys from his belt and unlocking the door. The door swung shut behind him, and Felyp heard the grating sound of the key in the lock from the other side.

He had to get in there. Perhaps he could wait and steal the guard's keys, or force open the lock… but anything he tried would automatically force a countdown to completing his tasks before he was found out.

No, he couldn't afford to have someone notice the lock had been tampered with, or to have the guard go missing. He had no idea what was behind the door, so he couldn't risk being found out before he had a chance to thoroughly investigate. He hadn't stayed hidden this long by being rash.

He glanced up at the ceiling. The rafters here seemed similar to the ones in the upper parts of the castle. There was only one way to find out. He scaled the wall, using the rough stones as hand and footholds, a task that had gotten easier and was almost second-nature to him now. He crept along the rafters, looking for the little trapdoor.

There! At the end of the row, the little alcove that indicated an opening. He crawled toward it and found the latch to open it, pushing very slowly, not knowing the state of the door or hinges, or how loudly it would squeak in this quiet.

At first, the door refused to budge, but with slow, careful motions, he was able to open it far enough to look inside.

The room was small, scarcely larger than a closet, and completely empty except for a candle in a sconce on the wall. Opposite the door, a staircase wound down into dark shadows.

Felyp considered his options. He could follow the guard down the stairs, but there was no guarantee he could find a place to hide, and the guard might see him. On the other hand, he didn't know what lay at the bottom, so if he didn't follow, then he might never know what direction the guard had gone.

The decision was taken from him by the sound of the guard's footsteps coming up the stairs. He remained crouched in the shadows, high in the rafters, breathing slow, silent breaths until the guard appeared in the little room carrying a small candle, unlocked the door, snuffed the candle on the wall, and left, locking the door behind him.

Felyp waited several seconds, until the guard was well out of earshot, before dropping from the rafters into the dark room. He kept a candle and a piece of flint on him for his many nighttime excursions into the bowels of the castle. He lit his candle and made his way slowly down the stairs.

At the bottom was another small room, a landing of sorts, from which three passages sprouted, two with stairs and one that led straight ahead.

Felyp paused in the middle of the room and listened for any sound. Finally, he was able to detect a light wheezing sound, coming from the center passageway, the one that led straight.

He crept down a long hallway until he found cells lining the passageway on either side. He listened again. At the very end of the row, he found what he was looking for.

He shined the light of the candle through the grate on the door and into the cell, at the man lying on the thin straw mat inside.

"General?"

Obedience

"Well done, all of you," the sorceress said.

Arna stood next to Jagur and the Healer in the little room where they met with the sorceress, and though Arna couldn't see her face, she could tell the woman was smiling.

"It's time to set the next phase of the plan in motion," the sorceress said. "I have sent a dove to my contact at the border. Very soon, we will receive the news that will launch us into war. Be ready."

The sorceress looked at the Healer. "You. Have you found the amulet yet?"

"No," the Healer answered. "I've searched the queen's rooms a dozen times, the treasuries, all the nooks and compartments in the throne room, everything. It is nowhere to be found."

"Keep trying. We need that amulet. We can complete our goals without it, of course, but having it will make everything much smoother."

Jagur bowed low. "What are the contingencies, my lady?"

"We have no need of contingencies. Things are going as planned."

Jagur stood, his face twisted in a sneer. "Oh, to be sure. Like taking three times as long as planned to convince the queen to marry me. Like the Healer refusing to die. Like—"

"Enough!" the sorceress bellowed. "The timing is unimportant. The Healer will die eventually, and until then, she is powerless in the dungeon."

"What if the queen continues to fight me? She still won't let me close to her, despite claiming to love me and be glad we're married."

"It won't matter. We have what we need from her."

"Do we? She could be a powerful enemy if she ever realizes what's really going on."

"She won't. And if she does, we'll kill her."

Jagur looked unconvinced.

Arna, too, felt the little niggling of doubt. The queen had proven herself far more resilient than anyone had expected. She had believed all the things Arna told her, because Arna had been able to seed enough truth with the lies to make them palatable. Her years of service to the queen had been pivotal in establishing that kind of rapport.

Years in which she'd gotten to know the queen as she really was, not this empty shell they'd made of her.

The queen was better than this. More powerful than any of them. They were counting on the fact that they'd subdued her, molded her into what they wanted her to be. Their plan relied on her total compliance, her total willingness to do what they said.

What would happen if the queen suddenly stopped being their unwitting slave? What would happen if she were able to get her own mind back? Her true strength?

Would she be strong enough to withstand Jagur and the Healer and the sorceress?

Arna shut down that line of thinking with a sharp mental slap. She couldn't afford to go down that road. Her daughter depended on her. Her daughter was her first priority. Her only concern. She did what she had to do to keep her child safe.

"Be ready," the sorceress said. "You all know your role. The next days will be vital. But now that Legerdemain is under our control, the rest will be easy. Go, now."

Arna followed the others out of the room.

"I really hate that woman," Jagur said.

"Quiet, you fool," the Healer hissed. "She could still hear you."

"I could do away with her. Finish the plan on my own." He grabbed the Healer's hand. "What do you say? Together, the two of us could do it. It wouldn't be hard for you to take care of her. She's no more powerful than Ada, and you incapacitated her with no problem."

"Ada was a trusting old fool who didn't see it coming. She—" the Healer nodded toward the room they'd just left, "is paranoid and sadistic. She would never take anything I gave her, and she would see any spell I tried a mile away."

"Who—" Arna choked on the words. "Who is she?"

The Healer shrugged. "I've never seen her true face. But I've felt her power, and it far surpasses my own. I wouldn't risk it. He knows, though." She stared at Jagur.

"I know that I have no chance of overpowering her myself. If you won't help…"

"We won't," Arna and the Healer said in unison.

"Very well." Jagur gave them both a curt nod. "We proceed as planned. As soon as the dove arrives."

They all separated at the end of the hall, going in different directions, away from prying eyes.

Arna scurried down the hall to the queen's rooms and let herself in.

The queen lay on her bed, asleep. The spells used to control her were sucking away her life, little by little. Not just her mind, but her vitality. The once beautiful, elegant woman was now a pasty, sickly waif, her formerly lustrous hair falling in straw-like strands around her wan face.

It was almost over. In just a few days, Arna would be free. She could go to her daughter, and they could escape somewhere together. Alive.

But what would become of the queen? Of the country? If Legerdemain went to war, nothing would ever be the same. Arna had lost her husband in a mining accident. How many other little girls would lose their fathers if Jagur and the sorceress got their way?

But those others weren't her responsibility. Only one child was her responsibility.

And she would keep her safe.

Jagur arrived a short while later. "I've just heard that a dove arrived from the south. The news will be coming any moment. Wake her."

Arna took a deep breath and nodded. She gently shook the queen's arm. "Majesty, wake up. The King is here."

The queen yawned and stretched. "The king? My father?"

"No, Majesty. Your husband. King Jagur."

The queen blinked a few times, orienting herself. "I had the strangest dream. I was talking to an older woman, and she warned me… I can't remember what she warned me now."

"It was just a dream, Majesty. Come, sit by the fire. I will get your tea."

"Just a dream. Yes, of course. It was just a dream."

The queen stretched again and stood, stumbling slightly as she made her way to her sittig room and sat next to Jagur. "You must forgive me, I seem to have fallen asleep."

Jagur smiled, that disgusting, slimy, patronizing smile. Arna's stomach churned at the sight of him. She would be only too glad to be away from him for good.

"It's quite all right, my love," Jagur said. "You still need to rest. Don't worry, I'll take care of you."

Revelation

"Your majesty!" A breathless Cadalanian messenger stood in the door of the sitting room where Terea sat with Lord—no, *King* Jagur.

"What is it?" Jagur asked.

"Winterborne," the messenger panted. "The city has fallen. Sunnland spies infiltrated the city and killed the royal family."

Jagur jumped to his feet. "We must go immediately," he said. "I can rally the army, but we will need your forces as well, my love."

Terea stood slowly. "Yes, of course. I will call Parliament to council and we will discuss the best way to proceed."

"There is no time for discussion," Jagur said. "This is why we have a treaty—so we can aid one another immediately. You must gather your army at once. And not just your army. Anyone who can wield magic, including yourself."

Terea stared at him, her mouth hanging open as the weight of his demand crashed down on her. Midwives and Healers, people with families—all conscripted to take revenge on Sunnland for killing the Cadalanian royal family. And not just them, but herself. She was compelled to go with him, and...

She grabbed his arm. "Jagur—I can't use magic."

He stared at her, his face paling. "Of course you can. You're the most powerful sorceress in the world."

She shook her head. "If I am, I don't remember it. I don't know the first thing about how it works or what to do with it."

108

"That's not… you *have* to. It's part of who you are. You should be able to feel it, as surely as you feel your toes or the snow in the air."

Terea closed her eyes, reached out with her mind, and felt… nothing.

"I'm sorry," she said, "but I can't. I don't know how to use magic."

Jagur sucked in a deep breath. "Never mind about that now. We must mobilize the army and the other magic workers. I'll see if the Healer can help you. Come on."

He led her to the Council room. "Wait here," he said.

The Healer arrived a short while later with a steaming pot of tea. "I've found a new recipe," she said. "The manuscript I found was hidden deep in your library archives, under magical remedies. It should open up the channels that allow you to sense magic."

She poured a cup and handed it to Terea.

Terea sniffed it, inhaling the strange, spicy aroma, and took a small sip.

Almost immediately, her body warmed, and her fingertips started to tingle.

Was that magic? She held up a hand. It seemed to glow, an ethereal blur that swam in front of her face.

"Good, it's working," the Healer said. "Take another drink, as much as you can." Her voice seemed musical, a soft lilt that reminded Terea of a flute, but dimmer, as though filtered through a shroud.

She took another sip and the tingling intensified.

"Your Majesty," the Healer said, her voice like the music of a magical dragonland. "Your Majesty, I need you to remember something. The night of the invasion, can you find that memory?"

A tunnel seemed to form in Terea's mind, dark on all sides, with just a pinprick of light at the end. She walked toward it.

Other tunnels and rooms seemed to branch off from the one she followed, but she couldn't see where they led or what was in them.

At last, she reached the light. It was a room—her room. A woman just beyond her middle years barred the door against the commotion outside, trapping Terea and a man inside.

Terea stared at the man, her heart filled to overflowing at the sight of him. He was tall, with blue eyes that sparked in the candlelight and a full beard that framed his face in a rich mane of golds and browns, with just a sprinkling of grays scattered throughout.

"Justus," Terea breathed, falling into his arms. "What's going on?"

"An attack," Justus said. "They came in with Lord Jagur's retinue. They're looking for something—an object of great power."

The woman at the door—*Mother*—turned. "Justus, move the table. We must barricade the door."

A lilting, musical voice floated in to Terea's mind from somewhere far away, down the dark tunnel. "Do you remember that night?"

"Yes," Terea said.

"You hid something that night," the voice said. "It has not been found. Do you remember what it is or where you put it?"

Terea's hand went to her throat. It should have been there. She always wore it. Where could it have gone? "I can't find it. It's gone. I don't remember where I put it."

"Keep trying," the voice echoed through the tunnel.

Terea returned her attention to the room, where her mother reached for a bowl.

She dashed some sort of powder over her own head, creating a cloudy veil that obscured her features, then used her staff to bash Justus in the face, sending him sprawling.

"Mother!" Terea gasped, just as the staff hit her in the head, as well. She tumbled to the bedroom floor and stared up at her mother, who unbarred the bedroom door.

Two people, faces shrouded under cloaks, hurried in, and Terea's mother barred the door again. "You're sure she won't remember any of this?"

"Nothing," one of the figures, a woman, said. She knelt over Terea and started forcing some sort of potion into Terea's mouth.

The other, a man, kicked Justus several times in the chest and stomach.

"I'm sorry, my dear," Terea's mother said, "but this throne is wasted on you. My people have suppressed magic because they fear its power— and soon they'll understand exactly why they were right to do so."

Terea blinked as her mother's voice faded.

"Did you find it?" the musical voice down the tunnel asked. Somehow, that voice managed to sound both soothing and demanding at once.

"No," Terea said. Her tongue felt thick, heavy, and her mind filled with fog. "It's already gone, it disappeared before this. It's not here."

The tunnel closed in and darkness overwhelmed her.

"She's waking up." The voice sounded hazy, like it was coming through a blanket. It was a woman's voice, older, but not ancient. It seemed familiar, but she couldn't quite remember who it belonged to.

She opened her eyes, then shut them immediately against the glare of a bright light.

"Terea, can you hear me?" the voice asked.

She blinked again, trying to find the source of the voice… but who was Terea?

Slowly, her eyes adjusted to the glare. She was in a spacious room with stone walls lined with elaborate tapestries. Gold sconces held unlit candles, and a fire blazed in a stone fireplace by the wall.

The bright light streamed in from a tall, glass-paned window framed with heavy, red velvet drapes. She was lying in a bed, covered with a soft, thick blanket, propped up with heavy pillows.

Whoever this room belonged to must be someone of some great importance. So how did she get there?

Three people hovered over her, staring at her with anxious faces. Who were they?

The woman brushed her face with her fingertips. "How are you feeling, Sweetheart?"

War

Arna stood behind the queen's chair in the Council room. The queen stared blankly at all the faces around the table.

King Jagur sat by the queen's side, holding her hand. "Her majesty has had a relapse. Her mind is completely gone, and the Healer does not know if she'll recover."

Arna bit her lip. She was almost done with this horrifying mess. In just a few days, she'd see her daughter. Then they'd escape. Go to Zyan or some other distant land, somewhere out of the sorceress and Jagur's reach. She only needed to stay silent until Jagur got what he wanted.

"This could not have come at a worse time," King Jagur told Parliament. "I have just received word that Cadalania has been attacked by Sunnland, the royal family killed. As per our treaty, Legerdemain's army must come to Cadalania's defense, and as the king, in the queen's incapacitation, I will lead them."

Sir Cristofer leapt to his feet. "This is preposterous. Does no one else find the timing of this to be suspicious? They've scarcely been married a week, and now we are following him to war?"

"I agree," Lady Linzy said, "but we have no choice. We must honor our treaty. The queen signed it."

"The queen who has no memory of who she is or what she has done," Sir Cristofer said.

"I resent the implication," King Jagur said. "I have proven that we were betrothed long before her injury. Furthermore, she was perfectly lucid and in her right mind, both when she signed the treaty and when she married me. Both her maid and her mother will attest to the fact that she was sound in mind and body when she made those decisions."

The queen's mother stood. "Absolutely. Furthermore, I believe this is the same choice her father would have made in this situation. We must defend our neighbors and allies against Sunnland's ongoing quest for world domination."

Lady Linzy looked at Sir Cristofer. "I don't see what choice we have," she said again.

"I will not stand for it," Sir Cristofer said, glaring at King Jagur. "I will not let Legerdemain be destroyed by you."

"Then you are hereby stripped of your title and rank, and removed from your seat on both Parliament and the Royal Council." King Jagur nodded to one of the guards who stood by the door. "Arrest him."

The guards looked uncertainly between King Jagur and Sir Cristofer.

"This man is accused of treason," King Jagur insisted. "Arrest him at once."

Sir Cristofer walked toward the guard. "It's all right. Do as he says. We will set things right soon enough."

The guard took him by the arm.

Arna watched, the sick feeling in the pit of her stomach sinking further into her, infusing her whole being.

At the door, Sir Cristofer turned and looked directly at Arna. "Find Ada. She will set everything right. *Everything.*"

Arna gulped. Did he know about her daughter? Would Ada be able to help? What if...

No, she couldn't think about that. And she couldn't find Ada. Ada was missing, and quite possibly the cause of all this in the first place.

But she knew that wasn't true. Ada was not the veiled sorceress.

The sorceres was someone who wanted to rule not only Legerdemain, but also Cadalania, and perhaps even Sunnland and Kir...

She choked back the realization. The one who never got to reign when her husband died, because Legerdemain rule passed to the oldest child.

Arna dared a look at the queen's mother, but the older woman didn't notice her. She was staring at Sir Cristofer, a look of smug satisfaction on her face as she watched the man being led away by the guard.

No, it couldn't be. Could it? The queen's own mother? Arna couldn't fathom such a thing. She would never do such a thing to her own daughter—steal her memory and sell her to a stranger, just so she could have a throne. And what for? The queen mother's life was good, comfortable. What would she gain by using Legerdemain's magic to rule other lands? Why could she not be content to live her life, peaceful and serene in this quiet, unobtrusive country?

And yet she had. The queen's mother had used her own daughter as a pawn to further her own schemes. And a woman who would do that could not be trusted to hold up her end of any bargain. Arna and her daughter would never be safe if they trusted the queen's mother.

Arna looked at the queen, her dazed, foolish expression uncomprehending of what was being done to her. There was no other choice.

This was war. Not against Sunnland, but against family. That made the treachery infinitely worse, and infinitely more dangerous. But she had to choose a side. No one could remain neutral.

And she could no longer help King Jagur or the queen's mother.

She lifted her chin, a silent rebellion against the plot against the queen. She would have to be careful—she couldn't afford for them to know she was working against them.

Not yet.

But soon, all would come to light. She mentally checked the things she needed to accomplish. She had to save her daughter, help the queen recover her memory, find Ada, and restore the kingdom.

Time to get started.

"The queen should rest," Arna said. "I'll take her to her room so she is not burdened by plans of war. Come, your majesty."

She held out her hand and the queen took it, smiling stupidly up at her. "It will all be well soon," she murmured.

Found

The footsteps sounded different today. Softer, more subtle, not the heavy thuds of the guard's boots. And it was the wrong time. He wasn't due to bring Ada her solitary meal for at least a half a day.

Ada checked her nest of mold. It was growing, but too slowly, and she was too weak to help it along. She absorbed the tiniest bit of magic from it, and funneled some of her own energy back. Too much and she would overwhelm it, but she needed a little to give her strength and help her keep her wits about her.

She covered her little treasure with her thin blanket and went to the door. A few moments later, the footsteps stopped in front of her cell.

"Hello?" a soft voice whispered.

"Who's there?" Ada rasped.

"I'm here to help. I'm going to get you out," the voice said.

Ada tapped at the panel that slid open when the guard brought her food.

The person on the other side of the door fumbled a bit before finding the latch to open the panel.

She blinked at the sudden light. It was just a candle, but she'd been in the dark so long, it still burned her eyes.

When her vision adjusted, she saw a young man—well, young compared to her, anyway—peering in at her.

"Who are you?" she asked.

"A friend," he said. "Are you Ada?"

She considered lying, but a foe would already know her identity. Besides, she was already half-dead. There was only so much they could do to her at this point. "I am," she said at last.

"I'm trying to open this door, but I can't find a latch or a keyhole or anything."

"There isn't one," Ada said. "It's magically sealed. Only a very strong magical spell will undo it. Do you know magic?"

"No," the young man sighed. "And I don't have any allies who can help, at least not yet."

"No matter. It will just take longer. Can you get in and out of this dungeon without betraying yourself?"

"Yes."

"Good. If you truly want to help, I will need you to bring me some things. First, food. They've been feeding me as little as possible while still keeping me alive. Good, nourishing broth, and tea. Bread. Fresh vegetables."

"Yes, my lady. I will bring them tonight. What else?"

"The queen has an amulet. A very distinctive magical jewel. Is there any way you can get to it?"

"No, my lady. I have heard of it, but it is missing."

Fear clutched at Ada's heart. Very few things could be worse than that news. "Missing? What do you mean?"

"No one know where it is, not even the queen."

"The queen would not let it out of her sight unless something very grave happened. The guard told me she'd been ill—is she recovered?"

The man shifted on his feet. "Yes and no. Her health is good, but she has no memory of anything before the attack."

"No memory? How is that possible?"

"The Healer said she hit her head."

"How long has her memory been gone?"

"A few weeks. She seemed to be doing better, but she suddenly got worse again. Her maid and the Healer have been caring for her."

"They took her memory," Ada whispered. She was wrong if she thought things couldn't get worse. This was as bad as the amulet being missing. Memory spells were extremely difficult. Only a very powerful sorcerer or sorceress could pull one off, let alone maintain it for weeks. Worse, if someone else was controlling her, they could force her to make a choice that would affect the prophecy. "Who is the Healer?"

"I don't know," the man said. "But the queen mother seems to trust her."

The queen mother. Something about that made Ada twitch. "The queen mother is overseeing everything with regard to the kingdom and the queen's health?"

The man nodded.

"This is worse than I realized," she said. "You're sure the amulet is missing, not stolen?"

"Yes, my lady. Because Jagur is still looking for it."

"Well, that's one small thing to be thankful for, at least," Ada said. "Very well. Food and tea will suffice for now. And at some point, I will need you to acquire a gemstone for me. Preferably diamond, and the sooner the better."

The man nodded and bowed, then carefully closed the panel on the door.

The missing amulet was concerning, but not so much as the queen's missing memory. And who was Jagur? And why was he looking for the amulet?

The young man returned a few hours later with a knapsack full of food and a jar of tea.

Ada inhaled. It was good, ordinary tea, the kind she might have with dinner.

She wondered why it was in a jar not a cup, but decided against asking. There would be plenty of time for explanations later. For now, she had to get her strength back.

She devoured as much of the food as quickly as she could without making herself more ill, saving out some for later, and saving several pieces of bread, which would mold most quickly, and a few bits of vegetables for her garden.

She gave a contented sigh as she passed the plate and jar back to the young man.

"How often can you bring me more?"

"At least every night," he said. "Perhaps more, but I don't know this guard's schedule yet."

"Good. Thank you. Work on getting me a gemstone. I could get out of here in as little as another week if we do this right."

The man looked at her, anxiety playing across his features.

"What is it?" Ada asked.

"It's just… we may not have that long. I just heard the king is planning to go to war, as soon as he can gather the army."

"The army?"

The man nodded. "Not just the regular army, but anyone who can use magic, including Healers and midwives. He's taking them all and marching against Sunnland."

The king. There was no king.

War. Why?

Ada nodded. There was no time.

"I need you to bring me some things, as quickly as possible. Can you remember them all if I tell you what they are?"

Guard

Felyp waited until the Healer left before emerging from the passage that led to the dungeon where Ada was being kept.

When all was silent, he crept down to the General's cell. "General? How are you?"

"Better." The General's voice sounded strong now, healthy.

"What can I do for you?"

"Just get me out of here."

"I'm working on a plan. I found Ada, but I can't get her out without magic. She gave me some things to get for her, so with luck, she will be able to get herself out."

"The queen can use magic."

Felyp paused. How much should he tell the General about the queen's condition? Getting out was the first step. Once they were safely away from the dungeon, hiding in a cellar with plenty of food, he could explain it all. The bare minimum was best for now. "The queen is ill. She can do nothing for herself right now."

The General heaved himself up and shuffled to the grate. "Ill? What do you mean, ill?" Worry suffused his tone.

Felyp considered a moment, but decided there was no point in hiding things if the General really wanted to know. "She cannot remember anything before the invasion. I believe the king is controlling her somehow."

"The king? What king?"

"She married Lord Jagur."

"I need to get out of here. *Now*." The General's voice was angry now.

"When the guard returns, I will surprise him and take his keys."

"How long until then?"

"A couple hours, at most. He'll be coming to check on you and make sure the Healer cured you."

The General paced his cell.

"Rest, General. We have a long day ahead of us."

The General returned to his cot, but Felyp could tell he was still tense. He almost wished he could force him to sleep, the way King Jagur seemed able to force his will on the queen.

"Rest," he said again. "We'll be free soon."

He waited until the General's breathing slowed, then crouched in the entrance to the third passageway. It led to another layer of cells, not quite as far down as the ones Ada inhabited. The way the stairs twisted, he thought all three were stacked on top of one another, the General's layer at the top, then the empty middle layer, and Ada's layer at the bottom.

He snuffed his candle and waited for morning.

Felyp woke to the sound of the guard muttering curses as he shuffled down the long staircase. He stood, waiting, ready, until the guard passed the entrance where Felyp waited.

As soon as the guard was in range, Felyp crouched, lunged, and tackled him.

The guard spewed more curses as he fell, landing with a hard thud which sent his head cracking into the stone floor.

The guard swung, smashing his fist into Felyp's jaw. Felyp's neck snapped back and he rolled to the floor. The guard still gasped for breath, and was slower to get to his feet…. But he had a club.

Felyp ducked and rammed his shoulder into the guard's stomach, forcing him back a few feet.

He'd thought the element of surprise would lend him enough advantage to incapacitate the guard, but the guard kept coming, swinging his club with one hand and his fist with the other.

The club landed squarely across Felyp's shoulder, sending him crashing into the wall just beneath the candle in its sconce.

Felyp reached up and grabbed the candle, then flung the hot wax into the guard's face.

The guard screamed and dropped the club, his hands going to his face. Felyp scrambled for the club and swung it at the guard's head. The guard toppled, twitched, and was still.

Felyp crashed the club into his head one more time, just to be sure, then searched his body for the keys. He tried every one until he found the one that opened the General's cell.

Every muscle ached, especially his shoulder. The fight had only lasted moments, but it felt like hours. He was glad for the keys, so he wouldn't have to try to climb the rafters.

The General stumbled out and paused to look at the guard's prone form, lying in the glow of the candle that still burned on the floor. "Help me," he said.

The General dragged the guard toward one of the other passageways, the one that led to the bottom level where Ada was imprisoned.

"Not that one," Felyp said. "Here."

Together, he and the General dragged the guard to the empty, middle-level passage and shoved him down the stairs.

Felyp picked up the candle from the floor and used it to light his own candle, then stuck it back in the sconce. A few splatters of wax and a few of blood marred the stone floor.

"Just a moment," Felyp said. He used the thin blanket from the General's cell to wipe up the mess. If anyone came down here looking, he didn't want it to be obvious what had happened. He then piled the blanket on the cot in the cell, to make it appear at first glance as though the General might be curled up under it, sick or dead.

Finally, he came out and locked the cell. With any luck, the mystery would keep King Jagur and his people busy until the General could formulate a plan for their next step.

The General sagged against the wall, so Felyp put the General's arm over his own shoulder, despite the pain, and led him up the long staircase toward the little room at the top. He slowly opened the door and checked for anyone who might be around, and when he was sure it was safe, led the General out, through the servants' passageways, and to the little cellar where he'd been sleeping.

He handed the General some food from his own stash, and the General sank onto the small nest of stolen blankets and clothes that formed Felyp's bed.

"We have to get to the queen before they discover the guard's body," the General said.

"You go to the queen," Felyp said. "I need to help Ada escape."

Rebellion

"My love, I must insist that you stay here for your own safety," Jagur said. His voice filtered in through a dense fog.

Terea nodded, though she didn't really know why. What was unsafe? She felt like she should know, but everything was so fuzzy. But he'd told her to wait here, so wait she would. She had to obey him when he told her things. She didn't remember why, but she knew when he called her "my love," he must be obeyed.

She sat on the edge of her bed—was it her bed?—yes, it must be. She sat on the edge of her bed and waited for Jagur to speak to the other woman in the room.

"Keep her here," he said. "I'll be back when we've dealt with the insurrection. I'll send the Healer with some tea."

The woman... a maid... Arna—yes, that was it—nodded and barred the door as soon as Jagur left. "How are you feeling, Majesty?"

"I don't know," Terea said. "What is the insurrection?"

"A prisoner has escaped from the dungeon," Arna said. "A very dangerous man. We fear your life is in danger."

A dangerous man? Terea tried to think who might be dangerous, but the only face her mind could pull together was Jagur's. Was he the only man she knew? He couldn't be... and yet she couldn't picture anyone else.

Something was wrong. Very, very wrong. She knew better than this. She knew she was able to think once—why wouldn't her mind work the way it was supposed to? Why couldn't she remember or figure out the

124

things she used to? They told her she'd been injured, but she didn't feel any pain. They told her the Healer was helping, but every time she drank the medicine, her mind felt further from her.

Tears stung her eyes, and she blinked them back. She could not cry. She was a queen, and she must behave like one. But how did a queen whose mind was broken behave?

The fog felt like it was lifting just the slightest amount. If she could only keep it clear for a little while longer, maybe she'd be able to figure it out.

A knock at the door jolted her from her thoughts. Arna hurried to open it, admitting the Healer, who bore a steaming pot of tea.

"It's time for your tea, Majesty."

"I... I don't think I want any tea just now," Terea said.

"Nonsense. This is what is making you better."

Yes, of course. The tea was medicinal. It was helping her put her mind back together.

She started to reach her hand out to take it, but stopped. Was the tea helping? If it was, why did she still feel like her mind was made of porridge? Why could she not remember details of the last several days—even weeks, perhaps. They'd told her Jagur had been here for several weeks, but though she remembered bits of conversations with him, the sense of the passage of time was mixed in with her porridge-like thoughts.

The Healer rolled her eyes. "I don't have time for this."

Arna hurried over and held out her hands for the cup. "I'll see that she drinks it."

The Healer nodded and went to the door.

Arna set the tea on the table and lifted the bar. "Oh, when the queen mother was in here before, she said she'd been feeling overly tired and worn down. Do you have something for that?"

The Healer sighed. "I'll see what I can do."

"I don't mind making it, if you'll just tell me what to request from the kitchen," Arna said.

The Healer rattled off a list of words that sounded utterly foreign to Terea before disappearing down the hallway.

Arna barred the door and turned to face Terea. "Now, for your tea, Majesty."

Terea scooted a little further on the bed as Arna came toward her. Arna wouldn't force her to drink it, would she?

Arna reached the table and her hand suddenly jerked, sending the cup sprawling. It clattered to the floor, splashing hot tea over the marble flooring and up onto the bed covers.

"Oh, dear. What have I done?" Arna grabbed a towel from the cupboard and began mopping up the mess. "Never mind, I'll just give you some of the tea meant for your mother when I get it from the kitchen. I'm sure it will be all right." She looked up at Terea and gave her a smile.

Terea couldn't be sure, but there seemed to be something conspiratorial in the maid's eyes, a hint of something like a shared secret.

Had Arna done it on purpose? Why? Because she'd heard Terea telling the Healer she didn't want to drink it?

Everything felt… wrong. But Arna was helping her. At least, she was at the moment. Could Arna be trusted? And why did that feel like such an important question?

A short while later, Arna called for a servant to bring tea for the queen mother, repeating some of the strange-sounding names the Healer had mentioned. She poured tea for both Terea and herself. Terea stared at the cup for awhile. Arna didn't push her to drink, only sat and calmly drank her own.

She'd poured both from the same pot, in clean cups from the kitchen. Terea sniffed it. It smelled good. Tangy and robust. She glanced again at Arna, who finished hers and poured another cup.

It must be safe.

Terea took a sip. The hot liquid spread through her, warming away the chill Terea hadn't even realized permeated her whole body. She inhaled and took another drink. With every sip, the heavy cloud that seemed to enshroud her mind seemed to lift.

"I think I would like this tea from now on, instead of the other," she said when she finished her cup.

Arna smiled. "Yes, your majesty. Although if I were you I wouldn't mention it to the Healer. You know how they are, always thinking they know best."

Terea nodded. There was more wisdom in those words than she'd considered. She had to trust someone, and Arna seemed like the best candidate. Somehow, she would figure out what was happening to her, and take back control of her life.

Insurrection

"Drink your tea, my love," Jagur said.

Terea automatically brought the cup to her lips before she caught herself and paused.

"My love, you'll never get healthy if you don't drink what the Healer gives you," he chided.

His voice, the cadence of it, made her want to obey. Even as she realized it wasn't real, that his words were some sort of spell, she still wanted to obey him, to trust him.

She swallowed, and glanced around her room.

Arna stood on the other side, waiting patiently, ready to help. They'd agreed to go on pretending everything was as it had been before she stopped drinking the tea until they were ready to put their plan into action, but Arna was ready if they should need to act sooner.

"It's… cold," Terea said.

"Allow me," Ara said, hurrying over. She took the cup and set it in the warmer by the edge of the fire. Arna kept her back to Lord Jagur, but Terea watched as she deftly switched the cup with an identical one that was filled with ordinary tea, and brought that one to Terea a few minutes later.

"Better?" Arna asked.

"Mmm," Terea nodded, sending her maid a silent 'thank you.'

She allowed her expression to go slack.

Jagur seemed satisfied. "I leave in the morning for Cadalania. Your mother will be here to help you until then."

Her mother.

Terea had a strange feeling about her mother. She remembered…
something, but she couldn't quite think of what it was.

She didn't trust her mother, but she couldn't quite remember why.

Arna gave her a nod. They'd discussed this. She was supposed to say
something.

What was it?

Oh, yes. "I would like to call a Council meeting. I want to be sure
they—and Parliament—know my wishes before you leave. In case… in
case my memory relapses again."

"A wise plan, my love," Jagur said. "We'll convene this afternoon."

He left her room, locking the door behind him.

"What do I do now?" Terea asked.

"In front of the Council, you publicly denounce Jagur and demand
his arrest."

"What if I can't remember?"

"You will," Arna said. "Start talking about him. And your mother. I
will confess my part, and they will arrest us all. But be careful. Your
mother knows magic. She may try to harm you."

"I don't want you to be arrested. You're the only one who has helped
me."

Arna smiled. "Once you get your kingdom back, you can pardon me,
if you wish. If not, I only ask that you keep my daughter safe."

Terea nodded.

She paced her room until Jagur returned to escort her to the Council
meeting.

Jagur took her arm and sat at the head of the table—*her* seat—as the
rest of the Council, including her mother, filed in.

Arna stood behind Terea, her hand a comforting warmth on Terea's
shoulder.

When all were seated, Jagur cleared his throat. "The queen would
like to make sure we have, in writing, her wishes for the kingdom during
my absence," he said. "I have brought a document, which we will all

sign, giving the queen mother authority in my absence. This document states—"

Terea stood, her legs shaking, her heart hammering into her throat.

"I would like to say something," she said.

Lady Linzy looked at her, a smile forming behind her eyes, though her lips barely twitched.

"My love," Jagur said.

For a moment, the pull on her mind threatened to block out everything else. She almost looked at him, almost let his influence change her mind. Instead, Terea focused on Lady Linzy. Her faith, her support, an anchor in Terea's swirling thoughts.

"I, Queen Terea of Legerdemain, in my right mind and with the full authority of the throne of Legerdemain, hereby publicly and irrevocably denounce King Jagur and call for his immediate removal from office, and his arrest, on the grounds of treason and espionage.

Jagur jumped to his feet. "My love!" he shouted.

Terea ignored him.

"I also denounce my mother, on the grounds of treason. Arrest them both immediately."

Lady Linzy grinned. "Guards!" she yelled.

Jagur backhanded Lady Linzy across the face, sending her sprawling on the ground, then swung at Terea, knocking her to the floor, as well.

Arna screamed, but her voice was cut off by a knife to her throat. Jagur's knife.

Terea tried to rise from the floor, but Jagur kicked her. Her mother stood over her, a blue gemstone in her hand. A strange, swirling blue light seemed to come from the gem and wrap itself around Terea, silencing her.

Power shot from the gem, slicing through the members of the Council. Terea couldn't tell if they were dead or just incapacitated, and she couldn't move. A moment later, the door to the Council room burst open.

The guards shoved their way inside. Terea tried to call out to them, but she couldn't speak.

"We have identified the traitor," Jagur said. He pointed to Arna's body, on the floor in a pool of blood. "She tried to murder the queen. We must act immediately. All the members of the Council, save the queen mother, have been part of a plot to overthrow the throne. Those who are alive must be taken to the dungeons immediately."

The guards obeyed him without a word.

Terea's mother stepped over Lady Linzy's body and stood next to Jagur. "What do we do with her?" She nodded toward Terea.

"Leave her here. This room is designed to be a fortress. She can't escape. We need to take the army and get to Cadalania before someone figures out what's going on."

"We can't just leave this place unguarded," her mother said.

Jagur shrugged. "Then you stay and rule. No one will dispute you. Have the Healer make a potion to destroy Terea's mind completely. We don't need her to recover."

Terea's mother sighed and nodded. "We should at least get someone to clean up this mess."

"Someone will. But not before I'm gone. When I return, the entirety of the continent will be ours."

"May Kir and his armies live forever," Terea's mother said.

They left and barred the door, leaving Terea inside with the dead bodies of those who had been her allies.

Spells

Ada flexed her fingers. The food had already strengthened her, and the extra she was able to put on her mold garden had made the little bit of growth expand already.

It wasn't as much as she would've liked, but there was no time. The young man—Felyp, he'd said his name was—had brought her everything she asked for. And when he had, he'd informed her that there'd been a coup. The queen was locked in the Council room, a room that didn't have one of his secret entrances that he used to get into other places.

A man Felyp called the General was trying to find a way to get the queen out, and King Jagur was preparing the army to leave within the hour.

Felyp had promised to return within the hour with a gemstone. She breathed deeply, feeling the magic charging the air.

Felyp had left the panel open, and she listened for his return.

An eternity or so later, she heard his soft footfalls thumping down the stairs.

Panting, he thrust his hand through the opening. "I stole this from one of the nobles' rooms. Will it do?"

Ada took the necklace from his hand and felt it, touching it with magic. Opal. Not ideal, but it would have to do. "Thank you," she told Felyp. "Now, stand back."

Felyp shuffled away and Ada took a deep breath. She had one shot at this. If she didn't do it right, she would burn away the magic and potentially trap herself in here forever.

She pulled at the magic from the mold garden and funneled a little back in, cycling it in and out, putting back a little less than she took with each cycle, until the magic flowed through her. Then, channeling it through the gemstone, she directed it toward the magical seals on the door. She could feel them now, feel where the spell was put together, and how it worked. It was fairly simple, really, and not very powerful as far as spells went, especially since it had been sitting dormant for so many weeks.

The magic shot from the gemstone and incinerated the spell that sealed the door, revealing an ordinary cell door, not even locked.

Magic flowed through her, fueling her, strengthening her. She pushed through the door.

Felyp stood a few feet away, gaping at her. "How did you…"

"Never mind that. Where do we go?"

Felyp turned and trotted up the hallway, pausing when he got to the stairs. "Do you need help?" he asked.

Ada smiled. "I'm in better shape than I look. Go."

With a nod, Felyp turned and scurried up the stairs. Weeks in a cell with almost no food had taken its toll on her, but there was no time for indulging in weakness. She ran up the stairs after him, only falling a little behind by the time they reached the landing.

"Just one more staircase," Felyp said.

Ada paused and breathed in deeply. One more staircase. She could make it. Already she could feel the traces of magic in the air. Once she got out of this dungeon, she would be able to draw on that power to give herself strength.

Only a brief pause to catch her breath, and then she nodded to Felyp to continue up the stairs. They arrived at the little room at the top of the stairs, a space virtually unchanged from when it was constructed so many years before. Felyp fumbled with a set of keys and unlocked the door, which opened up into a long-unused cellar.

He took Ada's arm and helped her down the long passageway that led to the main part of the castle.

Finally, they burst out into a room with a window. Sunlight streamed in and Ada stopped, inhaling the fresh scent of the air, pulling in the magic that permeated the atmosphere.

"Are you all right?" Felyp asked.

"Better than I expected to be," Ada said. "Now, where is the queen?"

"Still locked in the Council room."

"Very good. Let's go."

Ada hurried across hallways and through rooms, dodging away from servants and guards. She paused in a hallway and snatched a topaz from its setting in an ornate wall hanging and kept going. This time, Felyp was the one struggling to keep up.

She rounded the last corner to the hallway to the Council chamber, and nearly ran into the queen's mother coming up the passage.

The queen mother stopped and stared. "You—how did you—"

Ada took in the woman's appearance at a glance, her dress, spattered with blood, her hair in disarray, and a large ruby hanging from her neck. The exact sort of gem one would use to exert dominance.

"I should have known," Ada said. She pulled magic through the topaz and unleashed it toward the queen mother.

But not quickly enough. A blast of energy, of pure rage and determination, shot back from the queen mother's ruby. The two forces collided, the shockwave of them sending Ada sliding backward several feet.

She dodged the next spell that the queen mother sent. The woman was powerful, but she lacked any sort of control. The queen mother sent another blast toward Ada, clearly intended to kill, but this time, Ada was ready.

She drew the blast into the topaz, using the conduit to twist the spell and send it back toward the queen mother.

The queen mother deflected, and Ada prepared another spell, this one to incapacitate the queen mother.

Just as she was about to unleash the spell, something struck her from behind, something heavy landing across her back and sending her tumbling to the floor.

She rolled over. A man stood above her holding a staff. Who was he?

"I told you we should've just killed her," he said.

"I'll take care of her," the queen mother said. "You need to go. You can't be anywhere near when the rest of the kingdom finds out the queen is gone."

Ada's stomach clutched. The queen was dead?

"You'll kill her this time?" the man asked, nodding toward Ada. "And you're sure you can finish the spell to wipe Terea's mind completely?"

"I told you I would take care of it!" the queen mother snapped. "Go. Get our kingdom back."

Our kingdom. But the queen mother was from Kirland. What…

But Ada didn't have time to finish her thought. The queen mother pulled a devastating amount of magic into the ruby and launched it toward Ada.

Queen

Terea sat in a corner of the room, as far away from the death as she could manage.

Arna's blood seeped along the grooves between the stones in the floor, inching its way ever closer to her.

She pulled her knees in to her chest, tucking her skirt underneath her. The room seemed to spin, echoing with the screams of her dead Council. Or was it her own screams? Was she still screaming? She'd screamed so many times in the last hour—was it an hour? It seemed like an eternity. But it might have been just moments.

She whimpered.

Her mother. Her own mother. How could she not remember something so vital, like her mother being a traitor? Had she known, before the invasion? Before they took her memory?

How long had her mother been planning this? It must have been awhile. She had her own people in place. She was working with Jagur. How long had she known Jagur? He was from Cadalania, and her mother was originally from Kirland, but she had been in Legerdemain since her wedding, more than twenty years prior.

Terea twisted the broken thoughts around in her mind, struggling to fit them together. Her mother came from Kirland, a peace offering from nations at war. Terea's father, the king of Legerdemain, accepted, and Kirland had been at peace with Legerdemain since. But Legerdemain was politically neutral, so the alliance had been one of goodwill, not of political strategy.

Bits and pieces of history lessons learned as a girl filtered back to her. A war between Kirland and Sunnland had devastated the smaller nation of Kirland. They had been trying to work their way back to prominence on the continent ever since, expanding their trade routes and even allowing the use of some magic, by officially sanctioned users, like nobility.

Like her mother.

Her mother could use magic. A memory washed over her, of her mother striking her. With a staff. Her mother had caused her injury. Her mother had put the spell on her.

And the Healer. The Healer was not someone Terea had known before, of that she was certain. Her mother must have brought the Healer in to Legerdemain. From Kirland? Or from Cadalania? Jagur could have brought her, she supposed.

But the questions remained. How did her mother know Jagur? And what was the ultimate goal?

Her mother had said, "May Kir and his armies live forever." Kir, the god for whom Kirland was named, a god of... what? She couldn't remember. Legerdemain had no national god, though they paid homage to the Creator, since he was the one the dragons worshipped. At least, that was what she had been taught. No one had seen an actual dragon in hundreds of years, if they ever existed at all.

So her mother was taking Legerdemain for herself, and Jagur was taking the army to invade... what had he said? Cadalania? That didn't make sense—why would he be taking armies to take over Cadalania?

Of course. He wasn't from Cadalania. He was Kirish, like her mother. That was why they knew each other. Why no one had suspected when they corresponded and made their plots? They were using Legerdemain to propel Kirland forward in political dominance. Legerdemain would be a vassal state, a puppet...

A puppet. Like she was. Yanked along by her mother and Jagur, made to do their bidding.

No more. She would not let them take her country. Would not let them use her army to further Kirland. Would not let them kill any more of her people. She had to stop the army from leaving. She had to stop Jagur.

And to do that, she had to get out of this room.

She stood, stepped carefully over the bodies of Arna and the Council members, and made her way to the door.

It was locked, of course. Barred from the outside.

They thought they had broken her, but they weren't going to take any chances.

Jagur had said someone would be in to clean up the bodies, but he would be gone by then. And when they came, they would put another spell on her. Debilitate her completely. She couldn't wait for that to happen—she had to get out of there immediately.

She looked around the room for any other means of escape. There were no windows, no servants' entrances. This room was secure in every way.

She looked at the tapestries, the history of her nation.

Her gaze landed on the picture of the golden-haired woman.

I am coming, the woman seemed to whisper.

Terea stared at the tapestry. She was coming. But Terea couldn't wait for her, whoever she was. She had to escape, to get her country back before it was stolen from her completely.

Jagur had been upset. He told her she was the most powerful sorceress in the world. He was angry because she couldn't remember how to use magic. He had intended to use her in his army, to take her with him when he went to overthrow Cadalania, but he changed his plan when she told him she couldn't use magic.

But she could. She just needed to remember how.

She gazed at the tapestry. Somehow, that seemed to help her focus, as though the image in the tapestry was training her, showing her what to do.

Close your eyes. She could almost hear the voice, like a memory, seeping through her. *Feel the magic in the air. Feel it through your whole being.*

Terea closed her eyes. Energy seemed to tingle through her, infusing her. Was that magic? How could she harness it? How could she use it?

She pulled on the energy, drawing it deeper into herself. It strengthened her. But she couldn't remember how to wield it.

She drew on it and focused it into her memory. She had to fix that, first, so she could remember how to do anything else.

The magic seemed to come to her instinctually. She felt threads of it burning away the last of the tea and the spell that had controlled her for so long.

In a rush, her memories returned, so many of them she couldn't sort through them all.

She picked the one that she needed right now. Magic. How to use her mind to pull and manipulate the magical energy all around her, form it into spells. Ada, the old woman, directing her, step by step from the time she was a child, teaching her every aspect of magic use she knew.

Terea sucked in a deep breath of air and magic and smiled.

Treason

The amulet had gone missing. Where was it? Terea searched her memory. Her mother had been looking for it. Jagur had been looking for it. Everyone wanted the amulet, because it was the most powerful object of magical energy the kingdom possessed. Both a storehouse and a conduit, imbued with power when it was created, forged in dragonfire, and connected to the Legerdemain royal line.

Connected to her.

The magic flowed through her, pulsating from her fingertips. She could use it with or without the amulet, but that would make her focus so much sharper, her spells infinitely more potent.

She closed her eyes and focused on the amulet and its connection to her. When had she last held it? She always kept it around her neck, so when had it disappeared?

Her memories opened up to a day not so many weeks ago, and yet an eternity. Here, in this very room, with Ada.

Ada had shown her a prophecy, given her a warning. She'd read the inscription on the amulet, and showed her the connection to the words on the ancient parchment.

And then the messenger had come to inform her that Jagur—no, not Jagur. Jagur was a lie. The messenger had come to inform her that her true betrothed was arriving.

She'd almost run from the room, conscripting Arna to help her prepare. Had she still been holding the amulet?

No. No, she'd handed it to Ada. Ada must have hidden it, but where?

The tapestry seemed to call to her again. What was it about that tapestry? She knew something, something important. What was it?

She walked to the side of the room and moved the tapestry aside.

There, scarcely discernable from the wall around it, was a small panel. It could only be opened with magic, and it hid a secret compartment. Ada had told her of it years before, and she'd forgotten.

Pulling a thread of magical energy into herself, Terea directed a spell into the wall. The stone panel moved aside, revealing the hiding space. Inside was a sheaf of parchments. She pulled them out and set them on the table.

The prophecies. Ada must have hidden them in there before leaving the room.

Terea sifted through the pages. There, buried beneath an ancient prophecy, lay the amulet. It must've gotten hidden in her hurry to meet her betrothed.

She placed the amulet around her neck, then directed a wave of magic at the door, shattering it, leaving it a smoking heap in the hallway, and stalked from the room.

More bodies lay in the hallway. Guards, and… Ada.

Where had she been?

It didn't matter now. What mattered was stopping Jagur.

Terea knelt next to the older woman and placed a hand on her chest, feeling for life.

A strong thrum of energy pulsed out from Ada's heart. Terea pulled magic through the amulet and directed it into Ada, strengthening her life force.

Ada woke with a gasp.

"Your Majesty," she said. "You're alive. And you're… you."

"Finally," Terea smiled. "Are you well enough to stand?"

Ada answered by rising to her feet.

"Jagur will be leaving, taking the army to Cadalania. I must get to the stables. Will you go in there—" Terea nodded toward the Council room, "and see if there are any survivors? Heal those you can?"

"The amulet?" Ada asked, her gaze on the brilliant amethyst.

"Safe in the secret compartment behind the tapestry in the Council room."

"Good. Go. I will tend to the wounded, if there is any life left in them."

Terea made her way toward the stables. The courtyard swarmed with soldiers and horses, but also with women. Terea recognized a few of them. They had come at various times to learn the Healing arts from Ada. They clung to their families as soldiers forced them along at swordpoint.

Rage burned inside Terea.

On the far side of the courtyard, shouting rose up. Terea marched that direction.

Two men stood facing one another, swords drawn, as a crowd formed a circle around them.

"How dare you," Jagur's voice rang out. "I am your king!"

"You're not my king," the other man returned, his voice low and menacing.

Terea knew that voice.

She ran forward, pushing her way through the crowd. "Stop!"

Both men turned toward her. Jagur's face paled beneath his oiled beard. "My love. How good to see you looking so well!"

Terea thrust a burst of magic at him, sending him stumbling back. "Don't ever call me that."

The other man looked equally shocked, but in a happy, relieved way. "Terea."

Terea smiled, her heart filled nearly to bursting. "Justus."

She ran to him and fell into his arms.

"Let go of her," Jagur demanded. "She is my wife. And I am the king. You will both do as I say."

Terea released Justus and turned to Jagur. "You are not my husband."

"All the legal paperwork says otherwise."

"I was under a spell. Anything I signed will be rendered invalid."

142

"Who will invalidate it?" Jagur sneered. "By your own laws, you need Parliament to overturn any legal documents signed by the queen. And all of the Council and Parliament members are dead."

"The blood heir is still ruler. I will form a new Parliament and a new Council. In the meantime, you are under arrest for treason against the throne of Legerdemain." She nodded toward the nearest guard. "Take him to the dungeon."

The guard stepped in front of Jagur and took on a defensive posture. "I'm sorry, Majesty, but I will not arrest my king."

Jagur's grin spread as the other guards built a barrier between him and Terea.

Terea glanced around the courtyard, but none of the guards were familiar to her. Were all of her guards replaced with Jagur's men? Was no one left who was loyal to her?

"Now, if you'll excuse me, I have a war to fight. A war that I am obligated, as king, to fight on behalf of my allies. And now that you're feeling better, you are obligated to come, as well."

He was right. Until the treaty could be formally annulled, Legerdemain was still obligated to see it through.

But she would not let Jagur destroy her kingdom for his and her mother's quest for power.

She drew magic through the amulet and into herself. As energy filled her, she remembered everything Ada had taught her—every spell, every application of magical ability she'd ever learned. Her fingertips glowed from the raw power that flooded her being.

"Stand down," she said to the guards, letting her gaze fall on them, one by one.

In response, they lifted their swords and took a step closer to her.

Before they could move again, Terea lashed out, striking the nearest soldier with a blast of power, stopping his heart. He crumpled to the ground, causing his fellows to take a step back, eyeing her more cautiously.

"Surrender!" Terea demanded.

A soldier yelled and ran toward her, sword aimed at her heart. She struck him with magic, and the next soldier and the next as they charged toward her, until only a few remained, slowly backing Jagur away from her, protecting him with their bodies.

"The king is under arrest. Arrest him or face the same fate as the others," Terea said.

"Oh, Terea," a voice behind her said. "I wish it hadn't come to this."

Terea turned to see her mother standing in the doorway, her hands glowing with magical energy.

My Love

Terea stared at her mother, yet more memories flooding into her.

Fear and rage and confusion all warred within her. "I remember now," she said softly. "I remember everything. I remember doing what you told me."

Her mother smiled, but not the loving, doting smile she'd known as a child. The sadistic, hungry smile she'd worn the night she first cast the memory spell on Terea.

"You should've kept obeying. If you had, you'd be happily living your life with your handsome husband. Instead, well, I'm sorry my dear, but I'm afraid your rule is about to come to an end."

"He's not my husband," Terea snapped. "And how can you possibly think that was happiness? Trapped inside my body, my mind a porridge of thoughts I can't quite grasp? Knowing something is wrong, knowing I'm dying, slowly, from the inside out, but with no power to stop it, or even understand it? Why, Mother? How could you do that to me?"

"You already know the answer to that." Her mother lifted her hands and shot a bolt of magic toward Terea.

Terea pulled on the magic in the air and created a shield of sorts, to deflect her mother's spell.

"I see you remember at least some of your training," her mother sneered.

Terea created a spell to bind her mother, magical ropes that would immobilize her.

146

Her mother deflected the spell, immediately responding with another. This one, Terea knew, was intended to kill her.

Terea created a spell that would absorb the energy and store it in the amulet before it could refract and cause damage to the soldiers and civilians in the courtyard. "Mother, stop! I am your daughter, but I am also your queen. You will stop immediately."

"You gave up the right to be queen when you refused to do what is best for the country," her mother snarled.

"And what is that? Destroy our neighbors and take their lands?"

"Power, foolish child. What is the point of being a queen—a sorceress, as well—if you do not use the power you hold? You could control the entire continent, yet you stay in this tiny little pocket of land, insulated from the world, from the wealth and prosperity you could have."

"At what cost? People die in war. We are not poor. We are not oppressed. This is a good land, and a good people. I will not send them to war unnecessarily. I will not destroy our neighbors and take what is theirs for myself. I have been given charge of this kingdom. Nothing more."

"And that is why you are a fool. Why this kingdom—and all kingdoms—will be mine."

Terea closed her eyes and pulled in in a wave of magic with her breath. She centered it in the amulet around her neck and built it upon itself. "I'm very sorry to hear that, Mother."

Her mother prepared another spell, but too late. Using the power stored in the amulet, Terea sent a spell to drain all of her mother's magic, all of her ability to wield, to even sense magical energy. The spell drained her mother's magic and vitality, drawing it back and storing it inside the amulet.

Her mother crumpled to the ground, looking twenty years older than she had a moment before.

"She has killed the queen mother!" Jagur shouted, running toward her, sword outstretched.

Terea rolled her eyes. Did the man have no sense about when it was time to give up?

It took only a tiny amount of magical energy to render him impotent, his sword clattering to the cobbles, his limbs dragging on the ground like they weighed ten times what they did.

A man rushed from the shadows. She recognized him—Felyp. Yes, he was Justus's trusted friend.

Justus and Felyp attacked the guards who rushed to Jagur's defense, and those who did not fall to the sword, she cut down, allowing the magic to burn through them. She hated killing, but they were traitors. War criminals who had attacked her. She was a queen, and her mercy had to be tempered with justice and prudence, with a priority of preserving herself as well as her kingdom before preserving those who would destroy her.

She turned to Felyp. "Since there appear to be no guards loyal to me, would you please do me the honor of taking the role of captain of my guard?"

Felyp knelt. "It would be my pleasure, your Majesty."

"In that case, Captain, would you please arrest Jagur and escort him to the dungeon?"

Felyp nodded. He prodded Jagur with his foot. "Up, you. You're under arrest by order of the queen."

Jagur stumbled to his feet, still apparently weighed down from the magic that Terea had used to incapacitate him.

"I am still the king. I demand my rights!"

"You'll have a fair trial," Terea said.

"How can it be fair when—"

"When you killed everyone who was fair and unbiased in the kingdom?" Terea snapped. "You forget, Sir Cristofer isn't dead. You imprisoned him. He will be the head of the new Council, and of Parliament. I'm sure between us we can find trustworthy souls to hear the evidence against you."

Terea stood by Justus's side as Felyp prodded Jagur along with the tip of his sword. They walked toward the castle door, passing Terea's mother, still half-faint on the cobblestones.

"Mother, you too. Can you walk?"

She looked up with a dazed expression that Terea understood all too well. She bent down and looped her mother's arm over her shoulder and lifted her up.

She turned to face the small crowd of Healers and magic users still milling around in the courtyard. "All of you may go home. We still need to deal with the treaty, but I will do all in my power to keep you from being sent to a war. You have my word."

From the corner of her eye, Terea saw Jagur twist away from the edge of Felyp's blade.

Something gleamed in the sunlight.

Terea saw the knife in Jagur's hand just before he threw it straight toward her heart.

For half a heartbeat, Terea watched the blade hurtling toward her, before she drew on the magic at her fingertips and deflected it. Jagur lunged toward her. She dropped her mother and spun out of the way of Jagur's outstretched hands.

She didn't quite make it all the way. His shoulder caught her midsection, sending her stumbling backward, down onto the ground.

Jagur was already moving again, dashing toward his fallen knife. Terea lashed out with a bolt of magic, but it seemed to bounce right off him.

He turned and sneered at her. "Did you really think I would involve myself with sorcerers if I didn't have a way to protect myself? You caught me before I had a chance to activate my counterspell before, but now…"

He was using magic. But a spell that protected against magic wasn't the same as a spell to protect against other things.

Terea rolled out of the way and picked up a fallen sword, lifting it as she rolled and thrusting it toward Jagur's stomach.

Jagur's mouth opened, shock and horror written on his features as he watched his blood pour out, along the sword's blade, and drip onto the cobblestones. "My love…" he sputtered before dropping to his knees.

Terea pulled the sword out and thrust it into his chest. "I am not your love."

Fulfilled

"Who was he?" Sir Cristofer asked.

Terea sat at her Council table with Sir Cristofer and Lady Merithine, the only two survivors of Jagur's slaughter. Sir Cristofer had been in the dungeon, and Lady Merithine had been ill, and so hadn't come to the meeting that day. Ada and Justus sat at the table as well, to help decide what should be done about the treaty with Cadalania.

"Lord Jagur?" Terea asked. "He was a Kirish diplomat. I met him at the Cadalanian capitol, when I journeyed there last year. I only met him once. In a hallway, as we both waited for an audience with the king. That was the same time I met Justus."

She looked across the table and smiled at her betrothed. "Interrogating my mother has confirmed that he is a cousin. They had been corresponding, and when my mother discovered not only that I had met him, but that I had met another man, they formed a plan. My mother always believed her father, rather than her uncle, should have been the rightful king of Legerdemain. She always felt that her uncle was weak, using marriage treaties and trade agreements to maintain peace. She always wanted more power. She wanted to rule."

"So, since she couldn't rule by law, she decided to take it by force," Sir Cristofer said.

Terea nodded. "She wasn't content to simply take my throne, however. Jagur had already come up with a plan to take the Kirland throne. He would murder the Cadalanian royal family—not himself, but he was the one behind the plan—and framed Sunnland for the act of war. His plan was to attack while they were weak and take over Cadalania. But when he discovered that he could do the same thing, only with my magic users at his disposal, he joined with my mother."

"One thing I don't understand," Lady Merithine said. "You mentioned that you believed Whytni was killed because she knew too much. What did she know? Why did they kill her?"

Terea shook her head. "That may be a thing we never know for sure. When we interrogated my mother, that was one secret she kept hidden. But I suspect she found evidence that my mother was corresponding with Jagur, or maybe that she was practicing magic in secret. Whatever it was, I have no doubt that my mother killed her. She was a powerful enough sorceress to create the plague that killed her."

"Whytni knew about Justus," Ada said. "Very few others knew of your secret betrothal, and even fewer knew his identity. Whytni was the one person besides Arna, who they already controlled through her daughter, who had met Justus and could've vouched for his identity."

Terea felt ill as the truth of that statement settled on her. Like so many others, Whytni had died so Jagur and Terea's mother could seize the throne.

She looked at Justus. "They arrested Justus at the same time that they put the spell on me. They kept him locked in a hidden cell."

"Why didn't they kill you?" Sir Cristofer asked.

"They couldn't. When I arrived, Terea and I sealed our betrothal with a magical bond. If I died, she would've known it. It would've interfered with the spell they put on her, overriding it."

Terea nodded. "I suspect, also, they thought they might need to use you as leverage at some point. If I ever escaped their spell, they would need some other way to control me, force me to do wat they wanted."

"They couldn't risk setting off the precautions we had taken" Justus went on. "I knew there was a plot—I discovered it in Cadalania, when the king sent the treaty. The treaty wasn't the same one that Terea had helped to craft. It had been changed. As General of the king's army, it was only natural that I would accompany his diplomat—Jagur, who had integrated himself into the Cadalanian court—on this mission. I intended to inform Terea of the treachery, but they overpowered us before I could."

"But we've stopped it now," Terea said. "We will make it right."

Ada looked down at a piece of parchment and smiled.

"What is it?" Terea asked.

Ada looked at her, her bright blue eyes twinkling. "Oh, just confirming a suspicion I had. Nothing to bother about. Go on."

Something about Ada's eyes triggered a memory in Terea. Where had she seen those eyes before? Buried deep in the still-foggy soup of her memories while she'd been under the spell, she saw those same brilliant blue eyes on a much younger woman, a woman with golden hair.

A knock at the door interrupted her thoughts.

"Come in," Terea called out.

A servant opened the door. "Pardon me, Majesty. The child is here."

"Please, bring her in."

The servant led a little girl, no more than six or seven years old, with wavy black hair, deeply toned skin, and dark eyes to Terea.

"Hello, my dear," Terea said. "What is your name?"

"Manae," the girl said softly.

"Manae. That is a beautiful name."

The little girl nodded. "It was my grandmum's name."

"Your grandmum must have been a very strong, wise woman to carry such a powerful name," Terea smiled.

Manae nodded solemnly. "When I am a grandmum, I shall name my granddaughter Manae, as well."

"And I am sure she will be equally strong and wise," Terea said. She paused a moment. "Manae, do you know who I am?"

She nodded again. "They told me you're the queen."

"That's right. Did you know your mother worked for me?"

"Yes," Manae said.

Terea took Manae's dark, tiny hands in her own. "I have some very sad news to tell you, Manae. A terrible thing has happened. There was a very bad man, and he tried to hurt me. Your mother, who was good and

154

kind and brave, tried to protect me. Manae, I am so sorry to have to tell you this. The bad man killed her."

Manae choked, her eyes wide and quickly filling with tears. "She's... she's dead?"

Terea nodded and squeezed her hands. "Yes. I'm so, so sorry."

"Where... where is the bad man?"

"He's gone. He was punished for hurting your mother, and all the other people he hurt."

A flash of fierce anger crossed Manae's face. "Good. I hope he's dead, too." In a blink, however, her expression changed to one of panic. "What will happen to me?"

"You will stay here with me, in the castle. All your mother wanted was to keep you safe. Before she died, I promised her I would take care of you. You'll grow up as a noblewoman, and you'll never need anything."

Tears filled her eyes again, and she nodded. "I think... I think I will like that."

Terea smiled. "I hope so. Would you like to see your new room?"

Manae nodded slowly, and Terea beckoned to the servant. "Please show Lady Manae to her room. See that she is lacking nothing."

When they were gone, Ada smiled at her. "That was a good thing you did."

"Arna saved my life. It's the least I can do to honor her for her sacrifice. But we must move on. The treaty. What do we do?"

"As I see it," Sir Cristofer said, "the treaty is invalidated. The Cadalanian royal family was killed before you signed it. Jagur kept any news from arriving until after he had your signature on both the treaty and on the marriage documents, but you cannot make a treaty with a dead man, and the king of Cadalania was dead when you signed. I have sent couriers to the Cadalanian successor, explaining what happened. But, as the royal family was killed by Kir, and not Sunnland, there is no reason for war between Sunnland and Cadalania."

Terea exhaled. "Good. So we wait for word from Cadalania that says they accept our word, and confirm the treaty invalidated."

Sir Cristofer nodded.

"Very good," Terea said. "I have made arrangements to visit the Four Villages over the next few weeks, in order to try to rebuild my Council. When that is complete, will hold the trial for my mother and for the soldiers who were loyal to Jagur. Very soon, I hope, we will go back to the peaceful and neutral country we have always been. Am I forgetting anything else?"

Justus coughed. "Just one thing."

Terea smiled and held out her hand to him. "We will be married soon, and all will be well."

Ada rolled up the parchment in front of her. Was that the prophecy? The one about the decision she would have to make? And what did that small smile Ada wore mean?

Did it mean Terea had made the right choice?

Dear Reader,

Thank you for reading ***The Prophecy***. This story began as a collection of short stories that I published on the blog I write for, New Authors Fellowhip (newauthors.wordpress.com). I had no idea when I first wrote *Rendezvous,* the first story in *The Heir*, that I would grow to love this world so much and that the story would grow into what it is today.

This book marks the halfway point in what I have planned for *The Amulet Saga*. I hope you'll join me for the rest of the journey.

If you enjoyed this story, please tell a friend. Better yet, buy them their own copy.
You can purchase <u>The Heir,</u> and <u>The Defector,</u> and <u>The Silver Shores</u> on Amazon.
Please also check out my first full-length novel, a supernatural thriller called <u>The Breeding</u>!

I love connecting with readers. Please find me on Twitter (@avilyjerome), Instagram (@avilyjeromebooks), my website (<u>www.avilyjerome.com</u>), and Facebook (<u>https://www.facebook.com/AvilyJ?fref=ts</u>).

Yours truly,

Avily Jerome

About the Author

Avily Jerome is a writer and freelance editor. She spent five years as the Editor of Havok Magazine. Her short stories have been published in multiple magazines, both print and digital. She has judged several writing contests, both for short stories and novels, and she is a book reviewer for Lorehaven Magazine.

She loves all things SpecFic and writes across multiple genres. She is also a writing conference teacher and presenter, and she enjoys speaking to local writers' groups and going to SFF cons.

She is a wife and the mom of five kids. She loves living in the desert in Phoenix, AZ, and when she's not writing, she loves reading, spending time with friends, and experimenting with different art forms.

You can find her on her social media and on her website, at www.avilyjerome.com